WOLF PACK

ISABEL DARE

ISBN: 1496151720
ISBN-13: 978-1496151728

It was five days past the full moon, and Kirk was beginning to sleep a little longer, without the wolf's need to wake up in the middle of the night and hunt. But he still woke up much earlier than Leo, who was not one of nature's early risers.

Kirk rolled up on one elbow and watched him sleep.

It was one of his favorite moments of the day: waking up early to relish the warmth, the security of having Leo in his bed. Watching him as he slept, with one arm thrown up over his head and his blond hair fluffing up like thistledown.

It was a strange thing to realize that he had never shared a bed with anyone, not on a regular basis. The experiences he'd had with men were all short and unsatisfying, and Kirk had guarded his privacy like something precious.

His privacy, and his secret.

But now Leo knew his secret, and so did others. Other *wolves*.

That was the strangest realization of all: Kirk wasn't alone anymore. He had never been able to find other werewolves, or even any information to tell him more about what had happened to him.

And then, after he stopped looking, the other wolves found *him*, instead.

Kirk still wasn't sure how to feel about that. There was an element of menace, of threat, that hadn't entirely gone away, even though he had come to a truce with the werewolf pack. The truce gave him a chance to run with them on the three nights when the wolf took over—and forbade the wolf pack from entering his territory on other days and nights.

So far, the truce had held, but it was early days yet. And by its very nature, the truce was alien to the mind of the wolf, who preferred things simple and clear. Intruders should be challenged and killed, or driven off. A wolf pack was kin or enemy, nothing in between.

Leo snuffled a little in his sleep and

moved his arm away from his face. The clear skin of his forehead was crisscrossed with pink pillow-lines.

Kirk smiled a little, watching him with a rush of tenderness that was beginning to feel familiar, though the force of it could still surprise him.

"Mmmh," Leo said. He was still mostly asleep, though Kirk could tell from his breathing that he was surfacing, coming out of his dreams and up into the daylight.

The urge to kiss him awake became overwhelming.

Kirk bent close and buried his face in Leo's neck, kissed the warm folds there, and wrapped his arms around him.

God, he smelled so good.

A normal human might detect only a faint, appealing fresh male scent, but to Kirk, Leo's scent was overwhelming, an instant aphrodisiac. The effect was a little diminished now that the moon was new, but it was still making his senses reel.

"Morning," he said huskily in Leo's ear.

Leo smiled sleepily and stretched like a cat, yawning from ear to ear. "Mmmh?" he said again, a sleepy interrogative noise that required no answer.

He turned onto his side, nestling closer against Kirk, until his pyjama-clad backside came into contact with a part of Kirk's that was most definitely awake.

"Mmm...hello," Leo said, his voice hoarse with sleep. He spooned even closer, and Kirk's breath caught as he felt Leo's warm behind rub against him.

"Hello to you too," Kirk said, wrapping his arms more firmly around Leo's bare chest. "Tease."

Leo's soundless laugh vibrated through both of them. "Insatiable," Leo shot back.

Kirk let his fingers trail over Leo's abdomen, his touch delicate and just this side of ticklish, knowing the effect it would have.

Leo wriggled in his arms, and his breathing speeded up. "Aah—you know I—oh," he complained. "I can't think—when you—"

"No need to think," Kirk told him. He

pressed close enough to feel every wriggle rub deliciously against his cock.

"Had such a nice dream," Leo said when he'd recovered his breath a little. He caught Kirk's hands in his, bringing them up to his chin and kissing them. "About the claiming."

Kirk stiffened. This was a sensitive topic, and Leo seemed hell-bent on returning to it again and again.

On the full moon, Kirk had taken Leo in front of the entire wolf pack, establishing his rights to Leo in some primitive display that he only barely understood.

When the initial euphoria had worn off, along with the wolf's inborn certainty that this was right, Kirk felt ashamed. Leo deserved better than that.

Leo's trust in him was priceless, and yet Kirk had dared to set a price on it by exposing him to the gaze of others. Exposing something that was private and personal between them.

"Mm-hmm, yeah," Leo said, and there was a tiny shift to his jawline, bringing out the stubbornness in his features, even though his mouth was still slack with sleep. "Your back was against the tree, and you were inside me... mmm... Remember?"

As if he could ever forget. As if every second of the claiming wasn't burned into his memory like a brand.

"Yes," Kirk said roughly.

"Like a force of nature," Leo said dreamily. "Taking me over."

Kirk wasn't fooled; he could feel Leo's hands tighten on his own. This was important to Leo, and Kirk didn't know how to deal with it. He didn't know what Leo wanted to hear from him. Kirk had tried to apologize, and it hadn't gone well. Apologies weren't what Leo wanted, that much was clear.

"I—" Kirk began, then paused to swallow hard. "Leo."

Words didn't come easy to Kirk, but Leo flinched when he heard the gravelly tone in Kirk's voice, and Kirk knew he understood. *Please stop. Please don't make me remember what I did to you. What the wolf did to you.*

Leo turned around in his arms, bringing them face-to-face. "So you still don't want to talk about it."

Kirk shook his head, feeling strangely helpless.

Leo's blue eyes locked onto his, and a tiny smile quirked his mouth. "That's not going to work forever, you know."

"What?" Kirk asked, baffled. He stroked Leo's shoulders, relieved by that smile and trying not to show it.

"That look," Leo said. "Whatever the wolf equivalent of puppy dog eyes is. You're very good at it."

Kirk didn't know what he was talking about, but he wasn't going to dispute anything that brought a smile to Leo's face.

He kissed Leo's forehead, then the tip of his impudent nose, and then his warm, willing mouth.

The kiss deepened, and before long Leo was gasping for breath and wriggling against him again, agile and eager, his hands running over Kirk's back and down his spine.

Kirk lost himself in that kiss, pulling Leo

hard against him, chest to chest, mouth to mouth. He was falling fast and hard, down into a world of warm wet tongue and delicious, wriggling friction.

"Fuck," Leo gasped into his mouth, and then he was pushing his pyjama bottoms down and away, kicking them off with graceless hurry. "Fuck, you are—you make me crazy, you know that?"

He was so beautiful like this, warm and rosy, his eyelids still creased with sleep. Kirk kissed him over and over, pulling him close enough to take his breath away.

"I could say the same," he murmured, sliding a hand down between their close-pressed bodies.

There, ahh, Leo was hard and hot and ready for him, so ready—

He clasped his hand around them both, gasping at the pressure, the heat.

Then he began to thrust against Leo, making them slide against each other, and watching with satisfaction as Leo's face crumpled into helpless need.

He was so open, so expressive...oh yes, and now the moans began, rapidly climbing in volume and timbre.

Kirk had never been with anyone who was so vocal. He felt an obsessive need to catalogue every single sound Leo could make, from tiny breathless moans to gasping wails and curses. *Let me have all of them*, he thought. *All of them, forever.*

That wasn't something he could say out loud, not yet.

Leo gasped in his ear when Kirk rubbed his thumb over the tip of Leo's cock, spreading wetness there.

It wouldn't be long; he could feel the gathering heat, the pressure climbing between them.

Leo shuddered against him, moaning louder when Kirk changed his grip and stripped them both from root to tip. Kirk couldn't suppress the growl that rose low in his throat.

"There," Leo said, muffled against his shoulder. "Like that—harder—"

His breathing changed, became fast and

ragged, and then he bit Kirk's shoulder and stiffened against him, his muscles locking as he came.

Kirk pulled him close and rode out his shudders, relishing the way Leo's eyes closed and a look of pure pleasure spread over his face, making him look like a debauched angel.

Kirk kissed him again, then thrust once, twice into the slippery heat of his own fist—and followed him into bliss.

***

When they shuffled into the kitchen at last, disheveled and yawning, the morning sun was already spilling bright light through the kitchen window, making Leo squint.

Without words, they began to make breakfast, Kirk setting out plates and making coffee while Leo cooked eggs and bacon in one of the heavy cast iron pans.

It's beginning to feel like a routine, Leo thought. If routine was the right word for something that felt so comforting and precious.

Leo looked over at Kirk and bit back on a grin. Kirk's long dark hair hung in his eyes, and he was wearing a ratty old robe that didn't do him any justice at all.

"You look like a cross between a hobo and a sheepdog," Leo told him.

"Hmph," Kirk said, but the look he shot Leo from beneath the curtain of hair was not cranky at all. It was fondness Leo saw there, a secret warmth glowing in his dark eyes.

"I want to go into town today," Leo said, stirring the sizzling bacon. "Get some painting supplies. And hey, is it okay if I buy groceries this time?"

There was a pause, and Leo mentally crossed his fingers.

He didn't know how Kirk would feel about this. But he *couldn't* keep living on Kirk's wages.

Not if he was going to keep living here... which was another item on the long list of things they needed to talk about, if Leo could only bring himself up to the challenge.

"Sure," Kirk said, sitting down at the table. "You can drop me off. I need to fix a chimney at the Danvers's place."

Life really was back to normal, now that Kirk was doing handyman jobs again, Leo thought, with a secret sigh of relief at getting over this first hurdle. *Or as normal as things ever get around here.*

"When do you want me to pick you up?" Leo asked tentatively. He slid half the bacon and eggs onto Kirk's plate.

As he picked up his fork, Kirk said, "No need, I'll walk."

Leo blinked. "That's...look, I've only driven down to town once so far and that was on the back of Erick's motorcycle," he began. *Whoops*, not a good idea to mention Erick; Kirk's mouth set into a hard, straight, unhappy line that Leo tried to ignore. "But it seems like it would be a hell of a long walk back up to the cabin."

Kirk shrugged. "An hour, maybe. Don't worry about it."

Leo thought back to the route Erick and his fellow werewolves had taken. Down the long steep dirt road that wound through the forest in sharp switchbacks, back to the main road and into town...He wasn't sure, but he had a feeling it would take him a lot longer than an hour to walk all the way back.

Leo slipped a slice of toast onto his plate, then covered it with bacon and eggs. "Walking doesn't tire you?" he said carefully.

Another sensitive topic, Leo realized that, but he wasn't going to tap-dance around Kirk's sensibilities for everything. It was too frustrating. He wanted Kirk to realize that what he suffered through every month had some advantages, too. There was no need to be ashamed of the gifts the wolf had given him.

Kirk shook his head. "No need to drive at all, really. But people would talk."

So they would, yes. Leo had no doubts about that. Not in a small town like this.

And what were they going to say about Kirk and Leo?

***

It was another glorious fall morning, with bright sunlight filtering through the trees in a riot of color: orange, scarlet, and bright golden yellow. It made Leo's fingers itch.

An easel, he thought longingly. *A proper easel, and some nice big canvases, and a good supply of paint...*

Leo took the steep switchbacks very slowly and carefully. He shot a glance at Kirk now and then, but Kirk didn't look as if he was worried for his truck.

Kirk sat easy and relaxed in the passenger seat, his long hair now tied back neatly. He didn't even flinch when Leo took the curve of the last switchback just a little too closely, sending up a spray of pebbles and dirt.

That was a sign of trust that Leo appreciated. He didn't have a car of his own, and when he drove his friends' cars in the city, they tended to yell at him. *Mostly for driving like a little old lady*, Leo thought with a grin.

Little old ladies—like Nana, his

redoubtable grandmother—knew their business better than anyone, Leo figured, or how else did they get so old?

"The Danvers's place is on the outskirts," Kirk said. "Just park in the town center parking lot, and I'll walk it from there."

Leo nodded. Some part of him wondered if this was about convenience at all, or if Kirk was ashamed of him. Did he prefer this circumspect route, so none of the townspeople Kirk knew would see him getting dropped off and picked up by his boyfriend?

Leo wasn't even sure if Kirk even *thought* of him as his boyfriend.

So many questions still hung in the air between them. It felt like tapdancing in a minefield sometimes.

He drove into town, watching the stores and restaurants go by, and trying to see if any of them looked likely to sell art supplies. Kirk had suggested the hardware store, but Leo hoped there were better options. The town was big enough to be able to support a specialized store, especially since there were so many tourists around.

He was driving behind one of them now, a huge slow-moving RV with theme park stickers all over it.

"Do people come here just for the fall season?" Leo asked.

Kirk nodded. "Yeah. They drive through, watch the leaves turn."

Leo turned down the next side street at Kirk's direction and found the town's main parking lot, tucked in between two older buildings and a church.

He parked, and Kirk got out, grabbed his toolbox from the rear of the truck, and hoisted it onto his shoulder.

Then Kirk walked around the truck and waited until Leo rolled the window down, wondering what was wrong.

Had Kirk changed his mind, did he want to be picked up after all? Leo couldn't make out his expression.

But when Leo rolled the window down, Kirk said nothing, just bent forward and kissed him. In full view of whoever happened to be passing by.

His stubbled cheek scraped Leo's smooth skin, but his mouth was hot and hungry and Leo couldn't help sinking into the kiss, forgetting about who might be watching them.

"See you tonight," Kirk said in his deep, rough voice when he finally pulled away.

Leo nodded dazedly and stared after him, too flummoxed to say anything. Kirk would never stop surprising him, just when he least expected it.

Warmth pooled in his belly, and a glowing pride. *He's not ashamed of me. Of us.*

His lips still tingled with the imprint of Kirk's mouth.

***

It took a while, but Leo finally found the art supply store. It was in a little side street, close to the town library.

At first glance Leo thought it was closed —the window looked dark, and there was dust on the display of brushes and pastels—but when he tried the door, it pushed open easily, setting a bell over his head jangling.

"Good morning," Leo called out tentatively.

A light came on over his head, setting the interior of the store in a warm glow.

"Morning, morning," someone called from the back in a creaky voice. "Hold on, I'll be right there."

Leo looked around, and his spirits lifted.

The store's supplies were much better than he could have hoped: professional paints and brushes, canvases, Japanese paper...all he was looking for, and then some.

"There now," said the store's owner, hobbling closer to Leo. "What can I do for you, young man?"

He was a bent old man, walking with a cane, but his eyes were both kind and sharp.

"I need some supplies for oil painting," Leo said. "A good easel, some canvas, paint and brushes..."

"Oh, we can do that, certainly," the man

said. "Are you in town long?"

Leo swallowed, suddenly hit hard by that question.

"I hope so," he said, hating the way his voice wavered slightly.

"Right," the old man said, and his voice was gentle. "Not a tourist, then, are you."

Leo shook his head, not trusting himself to say anything more.

The old man's eyes raked over him, taking him in, while he found the supplies Leo needed, yanking open drawers and fanning out brushes for Leo's inspection.

Leo was reminded uncomfortably that he was wearing scuffed jeans and one of Kirk's flannel shirts with the sleeves rolled up, and that he still had to find a laundromat. And maybe buy some more clothes; he couldn't keep wearing Kirk's castoff shirts. They were far too big, for one thing.

But they smell like him, Leo thought rebelliously. That was what made it so difficult to give them up.

"I'm pleased to make your acquaintance," said the old man, suddenly reverting to an old-fashioned formality. "I'm Henry Wilkins."

"Leo Travers," Leo said, shaking his hand, which felt as delicate as bird-bones.

"Always happy to have more artists visit our town," Mr Wilkins said. "Lovely light here, don't you think? Especially in the fall. And you're seeing the trees at their best, too."

"Yes!" Leo said. His shyness fell away from him; this was a subject he could rarely talk about, but now he had clearly found a fellow enthusiast. "The air is so clear up in the mountains. Maybe that is why the yellows are so bright—some of the birch trees are just spectacular—"

"And if you wait one more week, the ginkgo trees will be changing color," Mr Wilkins said happily. "A beautiful delicate saffron yellow, edged with green on the lowest branches, and such interestingly shaped leaves! Like a living fossil. Oh, you haven't seen the ginkgo yet? Here, let me show you where they are—"

Suddenly, the dusty old store seemed to

come alive.

Mr Wilkins sat down on a stool and spread out maps and sketches of the area on his counter, and got up again to make jasmine tea for the both of them, and talked and talked. He loved the mountains, that was clear, and he loved painting the outdoors. Leo's heart warmed to him.

"Just hard for me to get up there, these days," Mr Wilkins said ruefully, rubbing at his leg.

Leo nodded, feeling a rush of sympathy. "I know what that's like," he said, and then paused, flushing a little. "I mean, no, I don't know what it's like for you, that was presumptuous of me."

Mr Wilkins smiled at him and blew on his hot tea. "You're a charmer, aren't you. Well, why don't you tell me what you did mean?"

"I—well, I was walking with crutches until a week ago," Leo explained. "Got my leg caught in an old bear trap, up on the mountain. Apparently I was lucky not to lose the leg."

Mr Wilkins's sharp grey eyes opened wide. "Oh, I'd say you were lucky indeed," he said. "Nasty old things, those traps. Makes you feel sorry for the bears." He took a sip of his tea. "So you're Kirk Anderson's friend, then?"

Leo sighed and stirred a little sugar into his tea. "This really is a small town, isn't it."

His ears burned, and he was probably blushing right up to the roots of his hair. As if he needed to give himself away any further.

Mr Wilkins laughed, a creaky old laugh that seemed to shake his very bones. "Small enough for gossip, yes. Don't worry about it, boy. I'm glad he found you, and I'm glad you're thinking of staying. We could use a few more artists around here."

"Is there, I mean—" Leo found himself stammering, and he took a hasty sip of tea to calm his nerves. "If we—if I stay here, I'm going need a job. Could you use any help in your store?"

Mr Wilkins's bushy eyebrows rose. "I certainly could, at least for the fall season. It's not that busy now, but just wait until the tour buses drive by, full of ladies who paint and sketch in their free time. They get me through the winter, I can tell you that for a fact." He laughed again, even more creakily than before.

Leo smiled back at him. "I'd love to help you out during the busy hours."

Mr Wilkins nodded. "I'll have to look at the budget, see what terms I can offer you. Come by this Saturday morning, and if the offer suits you, you can start work the same day."

"Thank you very much," Leo said, suddenly feeling shy again.

Mr Wilkins's sharp grey eyes twinkled. "Polite, too. Those ladies are going to love you, my boy."

He wrapped up Leo's purchases, all but the easel, which was too big and bulky to fit in a bag, and Leo paid with his rapidly dwindling supply of cash.

After saying goodbye to Mr Wilkins, Leo left the store with a spring in his step.

He could finally paint again, *and* he'd managed to land a job more or less by accident.

Now he just needed to find a way to ask if Kirk wanted him to stay.

***

Laden with groceries, Leo staggered back to the truck. He was almost out of cash, but he had fresh food and staples for nearly a week, and plans for a celebratory dinner—assuming he got the job at the art store, and there was something to celebrate.

His head full of plans, he was already digging for his car keys when he noticed that there was someone leaning against Kirk's truck.

Leo blinked. His gaze traveled up a tall leatherclad body, to a fall of long blond hair and a cool blue stare.

Erick.

"Get away from the car," Leo ordered. He had no desire to talk to Erick, not at all. And come to think of it... "You're supposed to stay out of town until the full moon. That was the deal."

"Oh, am I?" Erick leaned against the truck with elaborate unconcern. "My memory is just too fallible, I suppose. I simply can't remember dates. Tell me, dear Leo—" he moved away from the truck with the speed of a striking viper, and began taking packages and bags from Leo's arms, "—what did you do with my little present?"

Leo glared at him. His arms were too full to stop Erick from lightening his load, not unless he wanted to drop all the rest of the groceries, including the eggs. And he didn't have the money to get more.

"I threw it out," he said, biting off the words.

He didn't want to think about Erick and his *presents*. He wanted to go home and start painting, and the last thing he needed was more complications in his life.

Erick lifted up the heaviest bag, the one with the wine, and set it in the back of Kirk's truck next to the painting supplies, moving as gracefully as if the bag weighed no more than a feather.

Then he moved in again, leaning into Leo, far too close. Then he slipped his hand into Leo's front pocket and fished out his car keys.

"Is that so?" Erick said in an exaggerated

drawl that sounded almost like a cat's purr. He straightened up with a sudden smile, dangling the keys from his right hand.

Leo blinked.

He felt almost as though he was coming out of a long, deep sleep. Or falling into a dream.

Something about Erick's voice, and the gleam of bright sunlight on those keys...

"You're lying," Erick told Leo, and his lips quirked up. "I can smell it on you, you delicious darling. You couldn't throw away something so precious, and you didn't. Is it by your pillow? Do you sleep with it at night? Do you kiss it when Kirk's not looking and say a little prayer for me to come rescue you from that homely hovel? I could, you know."

"Shut up," Leo said, flushing with fury.

He felt dazed and strange, and it was an effort to find words. Erick's voice was doing something to him, but he couldn't think what it was.

All his senses were heavy and sluggish, and his hand seemed to move in slow motion when he reached for the keys.

Erick shook his head and tossed the truck's keys to his other hand, keeping them out of Leo's reach and making them flash in the sunlight.

It was childish and petty, a playground game that Erick seemed to be enjoying far too much. He was nearly a head taller than Leo, and his reach was longer, and Leo felt like he was moving under water.

"Don't be so harsh, darling Leo. Remember when you sat on my motorcycle, with your arms around me? I enjoyed that. Feeling you pressed so tight against my back...mmm. I'm sure you enjoyed it, too."

"You tied me up," Leo accused him, struggling for words. He had *not* enjoyed it, and despite Erick's expert driving, he'd been mostly worried he was going to die in a crash.

He grabbed for the keys again and missed. For a moment, he wasn't sure if he had two hands or three.

Everything looked strange and wavery, as if his vision was going offline.

"I did," Erick agreed. "And it looked *so* good on you. Mmm, yes indeed. I thought it was a pity that Kirk didn't keep your hands tied up in that leather belt when he fucked you. It would have added a little piquancy to the scene, don't you think?"

"He claimed me," Leo said with effort. "I'm his mate."

That was what mattered. Erick had no right to be here, shouldn't even be talking to him. Kirk would be furious...oh *man*, he didn't even want to think about Kirk's reaction right now.

Leo had offered himself up to Kirk according to the wolf pack's rites, and Kirk had claimed him for everyone to see. They were mated, even if the wolves were the only ones who knew it.

"Then why don't you smell like you believe that?" Erick said, his voice smooth and cool and infuriatingly reasonable. "It was a brave action on your part, but you didn't know what you were doing. You still don't. You're not a wolf, and you don't know what it's like for us."

Leo didn't know how to argue against

that. He wasn't a wolf. He didn't *want* to be a wolf.

Erick sniffed the air pointedly, his nostrils flaring. "You shouldn't be out here alone. You had sex this morning—" He sniffed again, relishing it, almost like a wine connoisseur taking in a particularly good bouquet. "—a little hurried, but sweet, and you enjoyed it. But he didn't leave his seed in you, not since the claiming, and the bite marks on your throat and shoulder have already faded. You're worried. You don't know what he thinks of you."

"Stop it," Leo muttered, flushing up to his hair. "That's not—that's none of your business."

He flailed, trying to grab the keys again, trying to smack Erick in the mouth for saying such horrible, intimate things, but his hands wouldn't connect to his arms properly; they just flapped around like stranded fish.

"You have reason to worry," Erick said softly. "Kirk has been a loner all his life. He's never known the security of a pack. He doesn't know how to love; he doesn't know how to treat a mate. He thinks of you like a possession, perhaps, but no more. And he has no knowledge of the savagery of his own nature." He slid a long-fingered hand along Leo's cheek, tilting his face up as if for a kiss. "If you happened to be wearing the wrong scent, he might break your neck."

"He would *not*," Leo said, glaring. "Gimme the keys."

"Are you sure you're in a fit state to drive?" Erick asked, still so reasonable. "Look at you, your hands are shaking."

"Fuck you," Leo said, then blinked, surprised at himself. He didn't usually swear when he was angry, but right now his vocabulary seemed to consist of crude, one-syllable words. It was unsettling, and he wished his legs didn't feel so rubbery.

"Oh, I'd like that," Erick said with a smile. "I'd take you up on that offer in a heartbeat, dear Leo. But maybe not here, hmm? Unlike Kirk, I prefer to enjoy my partner without an audience."

Leo blinked again, slowly. "So does Kirk," he said vaguely. A slender thread of doubt seemed to wind around him, drawn tighter by

Erick's words. He knew so little about Kirk.

Erick smiled, as cool and mysterious as a sphinx. "Is that what you think?"

He dropped the keys in Leo's palm, managing to turn the gesture into a benediction. "Drive safely, darling. I'll be seeing you."

***

Kirk walked up the dirt road with his toolbox on his shoulder, enjoying the fresh air and the warm, slanting sunlight filtering through the trees.

The chimney job had gone well, and Mrs Danvers had given him a long list of things she originally wanted her husband to fix around the house. "He's so busy, he never gets around to it," she'd said, smiling ruefully. "Why don't you start on these, instead? Let's say ten hours of your time to start with, and we'll see how far down the list that gets us."

Kirk was a little surprised by her generosity, but pleased as well. His rates were very reasonable, but people often asked him to do simple jobs for free. "Oh, while you're here, could you just fix this lightbulb, I can't reach it..." That kind of thing.

Sometimes he said no, but often he gave in and did it, just to help out a little, where he could. Sevenacres was a prosperous town, but there was still a lot of hidden poverty.

When he was still a mile away, he began to listen for Leo's presence at the cabin. It felt uncomfortably like spying, but he couldn't help himself. He needed to know if Leo was there, if he was safe, if he was happy.

He hoped Leo would never find out what a wrenching feeling it was to let him go into town alone. Kirk had done his best to mask the effort it cost him. He'd let Leo drive home alone deliberately, even though it was like hammering a nail into his own flesh to let him go.

It was ludicrous, and he knew it. All he could do was suppress the instinct that demanded that he protect Leo at all times. He couldn't get rid of the instinct itself, not without getting rid of the wolf. And as far as he knew, that wasn't possible.

Leo was outdoors, his footsteps crunching through the thick layer of fallen leaves. A creaking noise: one of the old wooden kitchen chairs. He was sitting down.

Now he was doing something...Kirk sniffed...something that smelled chemical. What did it remind him of?

Oh, of course.

Paint.

When the bikers painted his cabin with their club logo, it smelled like this.

But this time, it was a good thing. It meant Leo had been able to find supplies, to take up his hobby again.

Or was it *more* than a hobby? Kirk wasn't quite sure. There was so much Kirk didn't know yet about Leo. And Kirk had spent so much of his life avoiding personal questions that he wasn't in the habit of asking any himself.

And Leo hadn't complained, but he'd been obviously, deeply unhappy that he couldn't paint, that he had only that tiny box of watercolors and a sketchpad the size of his hand to work with.

Maybe now that he had proper supplies, he could be happy here.

Kirk quickened his step, eager to be home.

Eager to come home to Leo.

***

Leo was half hidden behind an easel. He had set it up facing the stand of birches overlooking the valley below.

Kirk walked up to him, circling round behind him to see what Leo was seeing. It was strange; as much as he loved the woods, he had never looked at them as a source of inspiration for art. He'd never even taken any photographs.

He'd seen tourists making sketches, of course. But—*face it, Kirk*—he hadn't been interested. He had dismissed it out of hand as something silly that tourists did, like picking unripe berries or buying souvenir junk made in China.

Now that he saw what Leo was doing, it

made him wonder where he had acquired such prejudices.

Not from his mother, surely. She had loved the arts, and even bought a couple paintings to hang in the cabin.

Maybe it came from his father's side of the family; they were all relentlessly practical and down to earth, proud of their blue collar jobs and full of distrust for anything they didn't know. Kirk was pretty sure that his father John had never seen a museum from the inside until he met Marilee MacDougall, Kirk's mother.

He saw that Leo was holding the brush up in the air, one eye squinted shut, and waited until he was finished with whatever he was doing; it seemed to require concentration.

Over Leo's shoulder, Kirk peered at the painting. It was clearly unfinished, but the color was astonishing. The birch leaves were almost more intense in the painting than in reality: a mesmerizing, glorious yellow edged with other, darker colors in the shadows. A patch of gold in the gloom.

Then Leo's blond head turned and he smiled widely, a smile of such surpassing sweetness that it almost hurt to see.

"Hi," Leo said.

Kirk found himself smiling back, probably looking like a lovestruck fool. "Hi."

With one more step, he was close enough and bent over Leo to kiss him.

Leo's head tilted up instantly, and their lips met. Warmth flooded Kirk's belly, instant arousal that always seemed to happen when he was around Leo—

And then he took in Leo's scent. Something he had deliberately waited to do, so he could let it flood his senses when Leo was within kissing reach—

Leo's scent had *changed*.

Kirk rocked back. He took a deep breath, almost choking on the harsh, metallic scent that surrounded Leo.

It was like being stabbed with a blade of ice. It sank deep into his heart, leaving no trace.

Erick.

Erick had been near Leo.

Close enough to touch Leo, close enough to leave his scent all over him.

And this despite the truce between Kirk and the wolf pack—the truce that stipulated that they weren't allowed to enter his territory until the full moon.

Erick had broken the truce, deliberately, blatantly. And he had touched Leo with his bare hands.

I should strangle Erick for this.

"What is it?" Leo was saying, looking worried. "What's wrong?"

Kirk's hands balled into fists as the wolf roared inside him. But he would *not* give way to the wolf.

He would not hurt Leo.

Never.

He'd rather hurl himself off a cliff.

"Your scent," he ground out, glaring at the ground so he wouldn't glare at Leo. "You smell like Erick."

"Oh," Leo said almost soundlessly, and

color rushed into his cheeks.

He stood up from his chair and faced Kirk with his hands on his hips, looking almost belligerent. "Erick said you were likely to break my neck," he said, his chin thrust out in that familiar line of defiance. "Are you going to?"

Kirk shook his head, even though anger and pain were warring inside him.

Erick said.

He couldn't believe Leo was quoting the man's words to him. As if anything Erick said could be believed.

What were Erick and Leo doing together? Did Leo want to change his allegiance? Was Leo planning to move out? Were they lovers?

"I won't hurt you," Kirk said. "Ever. I—"

I love you. He couldn't say it. He couldn't throw that in Leo's teeth, not if Leo was already thinking of moving on.

But I claimed you, does that mean nothing now? a part of him wailed.

For a long breathless moment, there was nothing but silence between them, and a tension that stretched like a wire.

Then Leo took one step closer to him, and now his hands were dropping away from his hips, reaching out. Reaching for him.

Kirk opened his arms, hope racing through him.

Leo stepped into his embrace with a long sigh.

They held each other tightly, Leo's hands fisting in Kirk's shirt, Kirk's arms wrapping around Leo's back protectively.

The cold metallic scent that belonged to Erick still offended his nostrils, and Kirk tried to concentrate on what his other senses were telling him. He took comfort from the warm weight of Leo in his arms, the sweet sound of his breathing, and the brightness of his hair in the setting sun.

He nuzzled Leo's neck, knowing it was the wolf's need to mark Leo with his own scent and obliterate the interloper.

Luckily, Leo didn't seem to mind. He tilted back his head, giving Kirk access, and there was a tentative smile on his lips.

Kirk bent closer and kissed him, deepening the kiss almost instantly.

You're mine. You're mine.

Leo's soft, warm mouth met his eagerly. He clung to Kirk with his hands tight in Kirk's shirt, his blue eyes shining.

But Kirk couldn't lose himself in the kiss. The closer he pressed Leo against him, the more he smelled Erick's scent, like a slap in his face.

"What else did Erick say?" he said in Leo's ear, trying to keep his voice gentle. "Where did you see him?"

What happened between the two of you?

Leo looked a little dazed, and his kiss-swollen lips formed hesitant words. "He...the parking lot. I saw him there." He paused, looking strangely unsure of himself. "He talked about—about—he took my car keys."

"What?" Kirk roared, forgetting to moderate his voice.

Leo flinched. "He gave them back," he said softly, still in that uncertain voice that wasn't like Leo at all.

Kirk stared at him. "He took your keys and he gave them back," he repeated blankly.

None of this made any sense, but what worried him most of all was the bewildered, hurt look in Leo's eyes. Leo should never look like that.

Even with his leg caught in a bear trap, even when he thought he was going to die alone in the woods, Leo hadn't looked this lost. He was brave, he was clever, and his brain worked fast as lightning, always. This was utterly unlike him.

Leo nodded in a wobbly sort of way. "And he said—he—" Leo paused again, closed his eyes as if searching his memory, and opened them again with frustration written all over his face. "I can't remember."

Kirk hated to see him like this. He wrapped his arms tight around Leo's shoulders again, ignoring the blatant offense to his nose, and held on. "It's okay," he said in Leo's ear. "It's okay."

"It's *not* okay," Leo insisted, wriggling a little in his arms. He looked up at Kirk, his blue eyes wide. "Erick shouldn't be in town at all, right?"

That sounded more like himself again, Kirk noted with relief.

"No," Kirk said, a firm denial. "He shouldn't. He broke the truce."

"That's—huh." Leo looked pensive and a little worried. "So what's going to happen now?"

Kirk sighed. "I'm going to talk to Brand. We need to sort this out."

Unspoken, he added, *or I'll find Erick and sort* him *out. Preferably with my fists.*

"Right," Leo said. His voice sounded flat, but now the expression in his eyes was sharp, alive.

Kirk was relieved to see it, though he could tell that Leo wasn't happy at the prospect of Kirk meeting with the werewolf pack again.

"But—" Leo hesitated. "Maybe not tonight?"

Kirk looked at him carefully. Inside him, some horrible, jealous voice was howling, *Why, do you have a date with Erick?* but he stifled it. Still, he couldn't help tightening his arms around Leo's shoulders.

Leo was still wearing one of his shirts, with the sleeves rolled up, and that made Kirk feel a little better. *I wonder if anyone in town recognized that shirt and put two and two together.* That thought made him glow with satisfaction. Leo wasn't ashamed to be seen wearing his clothes.

"Why not?" Kirk asked, as gently as he could.

"Just not tonight," Leo pleaded. "Every time you go out at night, I—" He paused, biting his lip.

Kirk could almost hear the words. *I worry myself sick.* He watched Leo censor himself, biting back something that he felt he couldn't say.

Kirk wished he wouldn't do that. Leo should be able to say anything to him.

"You know it's different now," Kirk said slowly. "The—change—isn't coming tonight."

It was still an effort for him to say the word, and Leo flinched just a little in sympathy, his eyes very wide and blue.

"I know," Leo said softly. "But I...well, I'd prefer not to sleep alone."

Even if Leo had thought for an hour or more about how to soothe Kirk's possessive streak, he couldn't have come up with anything better to say than that. Kirk took a long breath of relief, and he couldn't conceal the startled warmth that blazed from his eyes before they shuttered again.

"Besides," Leo said airily, appearing satisfied that his message had come across, "I have dinner plans."

Kirk smiled, just a tiny twitch of his lips. "Yeah?"

Leo nodded. "I want to invite this guy I know to dinner. He's tall, dark, muscular, devastatingly handsome..." He tilted his head back, looking up at Kirk from under his eyelashes with an expression that was simply *smouldering*. "Do you think he'll come?"

"Oh," Kirk breathed. "I should think so."

***

Leo sharpened the big kitchen knife with careful strokes against the whetstone he'd picked up.

For a man who didn't cook much, Kirk owned surprisingly good knives: old, hand-forged, heavy knives that were worth their weight in gold to someone who knew how to put an edge on them.

Leo had been taught how to sharpen knives by his grandmother. His Nana was eccentric in many ways, but she was clear-headed and ruthless about cooking.

"Sharp knives don't cut your hands," she would say, waving one of her favorites in the air demonstratively. "Dull knives do. Dull knives, dull food. Remember that!"

And Leo would nod dutifully, ignoring the fact that he'd certainly cut his hands on those wickedly sharp knives before.

Leo sighed a little. He missed his grandmother. It was hard to believe she was gone, when his memories of her were so clear that she could be standing right next to him.

I'll just have to do her proud.

With a twist of his shoulders, Leo shrugged off the flannel shirt he'd been wearing and dropped it on a kitchen chair. It was getting pretty warm in the cabin, and he felt fine in just a t-shirt.

He stroked the knife's blade along the whetstone again, then drew it carefully over his bare arm to test its sharpness.

Tiny blond hairs fell from the blade of the knife, and Leo smiled, satisfied.

Time for some serious chopping.

Kirk was seated at the kitchen table, his brow furrowed with concentration as he cut slices of ginger into tiny pieces with a paring knife Leo had already sharpened.

He looked up when Leo flourished the knife, the last rays of the setting sun glinting in the mirror of the blade.

"That looks dangerous."

"Oh, very," Leo said, smiling. "A menace to vegetables everywhere."

He set out the bowls of ingredients, then grabbed a cutting board and sat down next to Kirk. As he began to slice spring onions, the sharp, fresh scent rose up in waves.

Kirk sneezed. He made a face, scowling at the onions as if they had offended him on purpose.

Leo did his best not to laugh. "Sorry," he said. And then, with sudden curiosity: "How come the ginger doesn't bother you? It smells just as strong as spring onions. Maybe more so."

"Not the same," Kirk said shortly. As he saw Leo's crestfallen look, he added, "I can't— it's hard to talk about. There aren't enough words for scent in English."

Or in any human language, Leo added silently. He nodded, though he didn't really understand. It wasn't something he *could* understand, the way Kirk's senses had changed when he became a werewolf.

However that had happened.

That was another thing Leo was dying to find out more about, but hesitant to ask outright. It was so painful for Kirk to talk about this, and the last thing Leo wanted to do was cause him pain.

Warmth glowed under his breastbone as he watched Kirk painstakingly demolish the ginger. Before Leo's arrival, Kirk's food habits seemed to consist of canned food and simple meals: fried steak, bacon and eggs, cornflakes, beans, salad. Nothing that required much chopping or seasoning. Yet now, he had asked—actually, more like demanded—that Leo put him to work.

"I love your cooking," Kirk had said, which instantly put a big smile on Leo's face. "But I'm taking advantage of you. Let me help. I know I'm terrible at it, but—"

Leo's heart had melted, watching Kirk look away and glare at the wall in apparent embarrassment. "Of course," he'd said hurriedly. "Please, I'd love to have your help."

And now, Kirk was taking forever to chop the ginger, glaring at it as if it was resisting his efforts, but he was doing a pretty good job, all the same.

Leo quickly sliced the onions into tiny little rings, then grabbed another bowl and started chopping the garlic. He didn't look to see how Kirk reacted to the smell of the garlic. *Give the man some peace,* he told himself.

"So what are we making, again?" Kirk asked.

We. Leo smiled. "Potstickers," he said.

Kirk looked puzzled. "And those are?"

"Oh, you poor soul," Leo said, eyes wide. "They're dumplings, you fry them and then you steam them. There's no Chinese restaurant in this town? You never had these before?"

Kirk shook his head. "I think there was a Chinese place here once," he said. "When I was a kid. But we never went there. As far as my parents were concerned, eating out was something you did once a year, for a special occasion. I never really got into the habit, after."

Leo nodded, feeling a pang of sympathy. "We didn't eat out all that much, either," he said, "not after my mother died. But that was mostly because my grandmother was convinced all restaurants were unsafe."

Kirk blinked. "Unsafe how?"

"Rat poison," Leo said with a hollow,

doom-laden intonation, imitating his grandmother at her most portentous. "Mice. Waiters spitting in the soup. MSG. Aspartame. I forget what else," he said, returning to his normal voice, "but there were a lot of reasons. Mostly I think she just didn't like to relinquish control of the kitchen to someone else."

Kirk's eyes crinkled. "I see."

"I feel a lot of pressure," Leo complained, "now that I know I'm making you the first potstickers you ever tasted." He sliced cabbage into thin ribbons, pleased with the smooth glide of the sharpened knife.

"And I feel a lot of anticipation," Kirk said, utterly deadpan. "They better be good."

Leo laughed, giving up the game. "They will be."

He picked up the package of shrimp, opened it, and shook them into a bowl.

Then he paused, thinking back to another meal. "Hey," he said, "how do you feel about shrimp?"

Kirk gave him a puzzled look. "...Fine? Not allergic or anything."

Leo wasn't sure how to approach this topic, but he was determined to bring some things out into the open. "Yeah, but I remember that time I made borscht. You didn't like handling the raw beef. And there was something about the color of the soup, too, am I right?"

Kirk bent his head, his long dark hair falling forward and effectively hiding his expression from Leo. "Yeah, well," he said roughly, "that was during the full moon. And the soup looked like a bowl of blood. It was hard to —be human about that."

Leo blinked. Somehow he hadn't realized that. He was so used to the bright beet-color of borscht that it would never have occurred to him to see it as anything else.

"So I'm guessing wolves don't have any kind of particular reaction to shrimp," he said, keeping his voice light, making a joke of it.

Kirk shook his head, his jaw set in a hard line, and Leo let the subject drop. Instead, he gave Kirk the bowl of shrimp. "Would you check these for me, make sure there's no pieces of shell left on them?"

"Sure," Kirk said, and with that, things

were on an even keel again.

Leo finished prepping all the ingredients, chopped up the shrimp, and made a dipping sauce. He'd bought a lot of sauce bottles at the grocery store: soy sauce, fish sauce, chilli sauce. Might as well use them.

Then he opened the package of dumpling wrappers and began to fold the dumplings, folding the dough smoothly together over a lump of filling.

Kirk watched with fascination, following every movement of Leo's fingers as he made the pleats to crimp the dumpling closed. When he was finished, the dumpling looked like a plump little half moon, with a row of tiny pleats holding it shut.

"These are supposed to bring good luck and tons of money," Leo said. "I don't know why, but that's what I was told." He smiled. "I hope it works, I have a job interview tomorrow."

Kirk looked up at him, away from the busy movement of his fingers. "For what job?"

"Assisting at the art store," Leo said with a self-deprecating twist of his lips. "I know it's not amazing or anything, but—"

Kirk shook his head. "No, that sounds perfect. I didn't even know we *had* an art store."

"You wanted me to buy my brushes at the hardware store," Leo accused fondly.

Kirk shrugged. "Hey, I know they have some."

"Yeah, for painting walls," Leo agreed. "But okay, it's possible I could have found what I needed there, too. I'm just glad I found this place instead. And I liked the owner."

"What's his name?" Kirk asked.

"Henry Wilkins." As they talked, Leo kept folding and pleating more and more dumplings, filling up an entire plate with them, all neatly lined up in concentric circles.

"Huh, I know him," Kirk said. "Didn't know he had a store." At Leo's questioning look, he added, "Cleaned out his attic some time ago. He's okay, but you better negotiate hard."

"Oh yeah?" Leo said, putting another dumpling on the plate. "Tight-fisted, is he?"

Kirk nodded. "I needed to hold him upside down and shake the money out of him."

Leo finished the last dumpling and eyed Kirk dubiously. "You're joking, right."

Kirk gave him a deadpan look, edged with just a hint of smirk. "Would I do that?"

Leo grinned.

***

"Those were amazing," Kirk said, pushing away his plate with a sigh. It was so empty it looked almost clean, and Kirk had to resist the temptation to lick off the few drops of dipping sauce.

Leo's smile was wide and pleased, and it lit a small fire in Kirk's belly.

It wasn't just how beautiful Leo looked when he smiled like that. It was the way he ducked his head and almost seemed embarrassed with the praise, as if it rarely happened that anyone properly appreciated his cooking skills. As if he wasn't used to being praised.

Given the things Leo had said about his

father, maybe that was true.

Kirk wasn't the best at expressing himself, either. But he was damn well going to try, if he could bring those smiles out more often.

Looking out the kitchen window, Kirk was startled to realize that it was dark out. He'd lost track of time, but it must have taken two hours at least to make the potstickers.

He wasn't used to food that took that long to prepare—it wasn't as easy as opening a can and heating it up, that was for sure—but he was coming to realize that there was a reason why some people liked cooking from scratch.

Ever since Leo had come to live with him, Kirk was eating like a king.

Maybe the work would have gone faster if Leo had better help, he thought guiltily, and then decided that it didn't matter. He was good with his hands, he could get better at this. As long as Leo wanted to cook for him, he would do his best.

Leo followed his gaze, looking over his shoulder, and a hint of worry crept into his expression. "You're not going out to meet the wolf pack tonight, right?"

Kirk pushed back his chair, which creaked as though it was going to collapse, and stretched his legs. Then he shook his head. "I'm too full to move."

He couldn't put this confrontation off forever—if Erick felt confident enough to come into town, to waylay Leo, then he had to be put down, and fast—but if it made Leo feel better, he could put it off for one night and meet with the wolves in the daytime.

Leo's face cleared, and he smiled again. "Good. That was my subtle plan all along, you realize."

Kirk smiled back, not without effort, and saw an answering warmth in Leo's eyes.

Leo was so beautiful. And it wasn't just looks; it was the brightness of his spirit that shone from his eyes.

Listen to yourself. You're a lovestruck fool.

Maybe he was, but was that a bad thing?

Leo bent to untie his sneakers, then

shoved his chair back and stood up, barefoot. He stacked up the dishes and cutlery, put them in the sink for later, and turned back to Kirk, stretching until his t-shirt rode up, and exposing a tempting stretch of bare belly.

Kirk couldn't keep his eyes away from that little strip of naked skin. When he finally looked up at Leo's face again, he saw that Leo was blushing.

Ah, so you're doing it on purpose, Kirk thought.

Leo's blushes were one of the most charming things about him. He was so fair that his skin flushed easily, and they were like a weathervane for Leo's moods.

"Are you *really* to full to move?" Leo asked, in a low sultry voice that hit Kirk like a punch to the midriff.

Kirk slid his eyes half-shut, waiting to see how far Leo would go. "Yeah, I think so."

"Mmm," Leo said softly, sliding one hand down to his bare belly, then tugging at the hem of his t-shirt so it rode up even higher. "That's a pity."

Kirk stole a look at Leo from under his lashes. It was getting more and more difficult to pretend to be relaxed.

Leo leaned on the table, his hips canted at a provocative angle. His hand stole higher, hiking up his t-shirt until it exposed his nipples. It only took a gentle touch of his fingers to bring them erect into pink little peaks, just begging to be nipped and nuzzled.

Kirk's mouth went dry.

"I guess I'll have to please myself, then," Leo said in that same soft sultry voice.

His fingers stroked over his chest, circling his nipples.

"You see, I'm very—sensitive—right *here* —"

Leo pinched his left nipple between his fingers and gave a little gasp that Kirk could feel all the way down to his bones.

"And also—here—"

The other nipple got the same treatment, and Leo's gasp was a little louder this time, deliberately dirty.

Kirk set his jaw and tried to keep still, tried to keep from shifting his hips, even though he was growing rock-hard. He wanted to see how far Leo would take this.

"And as nice as this is, I've been thinking," Leo said dreamily, "that it's been a long time since I felt—mmm—" he paused, rubbing his nipples until they tightened even more, "—since I felt your cock—" he drew out the moment even more, licking his bottom lip with a pensive air.

Kirk couldn't breathe.

"—since I felt your cock inside me."

Kirk sucked in a breath that rasped in his throat.

It was true. He had deliberately avoided that act since the claiming.

The claiming had been—not fast, no, definitely not that, but almost violent in its intensity. The memories he had of it were searingly bright, like a fever dream.

Leo, bare and on his knees, presenting himself to Kirk to be mounted.

The feel of him, so tight around Kirk's cock, his body shaking as he was opened with sheer unrelenting pressure.

The way Leo urged him on with breathless, gasping little cries, even as the entire wolf pack circled around them to watch.

Kirk had barely been able to keep to his feet, and in the end, he'd staggered to a tree to lend him some support as he lifted Leo into the air to be fucked.

It was the most intense, most amazing sex of his life.

And for days afterward, Leo carried the bruises and bite marks, until they slowly faded and Kirk could breathe easier. With the guilt came a dose of shame, because part of him didn't exactly relish seeing those marks disappear.

He *wanted* to see Leo marked like that.

Surely that was the worst side of himself.

He wanted Leo to be marked as *his*, to carry his scent and his seed and his marks for all to see.

It was unconscionable. It was pure animal instinct. No human being could want to be treated like that.

And Leo was, after all, still human.

Leo would never want to be a wolf.

Kirk shivered, watching as Leo canted his hips even more, tilting them toward Kirk.

Then, with a breathy little gasp, he began to undo the buttons of his jeans.

One by one by one.

Kirk watched, mesmerized. He'd given himself away with his harsh breathing. He couldn't pretend to be half-asleep anymore; he might as well watch.

His cock throbbed against the seam of his jeans, urgently, insistently. But he stayed still, his hands clenching a little, and he watched as Leo slipped out of his jeans as smoothly as a dancer. His injured leg was still bandaged, but it didn't seem to be troubling him anymore; it certainly didn't seem to inhibit his movements.

Underneath, Leo was wearing a pair of boxer briefs that Kirk hadn't seen before. They looked...intriguing, a dark scarlet in a shimmering fabric that did nothing to hide the swelling hardness beneath.

Leo smiled at him. Not one of those wide guileless happy smiles, but a little sexy quirk of his lips. "Bought some things today. You like them? They're silk."

Kirk nodded, feeling like his voice had gotten stuck in his throat.

The fabric looked so soft. Such a sensory contrast to the hard warm flesh it concealed.

His hands were itching to touch, to hold, to explore. But with a tremendous effort, he kept them still.

Leo tugged his t-shirt over his head and took it off, flinging it onto the bare kitchen table.

Now he was naked but for the scarlet silk briefs, his bare chest gleaming in the kitchen's overhead light. He was so blond that there was only a faint sprinkling of barely visible hair on his smooth skin.

Kirk felt incredibly overdressed all of a sudden. Overdressed and overheated.

He breathed slowly, watching Leo with the focused intent gaze of a predator.

Leo stepped closer, leaning against the edge of the table.

Close enough to touch.

"If you're just going to sit there," Leo murmured, "then I'm going to have to—insist—"

He took one more step, bringing him up against Kirk.

Leo's bare, warm skin pressed against him, chest to hip, and his face was flushed, his mouth half-open and sinfully kissable.

Kirk groaned, deep in his throat, as he felt the last of his defenses give way. He reached out and grasped Leo's firm behind in both hands, kneading his ass through the silk. It felt just as fantastic as it looked.

Leo's head tipped back and he gave a little gasping moan.

Oh, *yes.*

Kirk felt all his defenses give way in one fell swoop. He pushed Leo closer against him, then slipped his fingers below the band of the silk briefs and onto warm, bare skin.

Leo moaned again, and Kirk bent forward and licked a stripe up his bare chest.

Mine.

He wondered for a moment if he should stay seated. It would be satisfying to pick Leo up and throw him over his shoulder in a caveman carry, then deposit him on the bed in Kirk's room, like a delicious morsel ready and ripe for devouring.

Mmm. No. Leo had started this here, in the kitchen.

They would finish it here, too.

***

Leo wriggled under his hands, which only pushed more delicious, warm skin into his reach.

Kirk held on.

"No, hang on, just a second—" Leo was saying, but Kirk didn't really pay attention.

He was lost in the scented steam rising off Leo, a heady mix of pheromones that went straight into his hind-brain, stopping thought as effectively as a lightning bolt.

God, it was no wonder Leo's scent was enough to draw a whole pack of werewolves into the area. It was unbelievably arousing.

He bent his head to lick at Leo's chest again, using long satisfying swipes of his tongue.

"Kirk!" Leo smacked him on the arm, hard enough to sting.

He blinked, coming back to what passed for awareness. "Mmm?"

"Let me go for a second," Leo commanded.

It was an effort, but Kirk finally managed to let go of his warm armful.

"Man but you are singleminded when you get going," Leo complained fondly, moving out of reach and rummaging in a kitchen drawer.

Kirk just watched him. "And you're a tease," he muttered under his breath.

Leo turned back to him, grinning, a small

bottle in the palm of his hand. "I heard that."

"Prove me wrong," Kirk said calmly.

In answer, Leo simply shucked off the silk briefs and climbed on top of him, naked and hard.

Kirk sucked in a breath. The sudden weight of Leo sitting on his lap was as delicious as it was—confining. His cock strained against his jeans, pressing against the seam.

Leo bent forward a little and kissed him, a quick touch of those lush lips, then a slower, deeper kiss.

Kirk sank into the kiss, wrapping his arms around Leo with a satisfied sigh.

Never let you go.

Their tongues stroked each other wetly, and Leo seemed to go bonelesss against him, so warm and close. His hands were in Kirk's long dark hair, combing through it slowly, playing with his curls.

"I love your hair," Leo breathed in his ear. "It's so like you. It's wild."

Kirk kissed his impudent little nose and

smiled. He wasn't the one who was wild at the moment: that was Leo, seducing him with all the irresistible force of his charm.

Sighing with pleasure, Leo rubbed up against him, shamelessly pressing himself into Kirk's chest like a cat demanding attention.

"You're very impatient," Kirk said, hiding a grin.

He loved this, he loved Leo's lack of inhibition that let him straddle Kirk's lap buck naked in the middle of the kitchen. *Good thing I don't live in the suburbs*, Kirk thought. *No neighbors.* He could almost pity them for missing the show.

"Oh, you have no idea how impatient I am," Leo breathed. "I want you so much."

Kirk's own breath was beginning to stutter with need, and Leo's words weren't helping.

Shifting, Leo managed to sit back far enough that he could undo Kirk's zipper. His hands delved into Kirk's jeans, and Kirk's head tipped back with pleasure as Leo quickly uncovered him. His fingers were warm and deft, and Kirk couldn't help pushing into them a little.

"You're so big," Leo said, biting his bottom lip as he freed Kirk's erection from his jeans and underwear. "Fuck. I love how big you are, look at you."

Kirk bit back a groan as Leo's clever fingers stripped him from root to tip.

He felt himself grow even harder. It felt incredibly dirty, sitting here like this, completely dressed with just his dick bare, springing up from his undone jeans like a flagpole. And Leo, half leaning against the table, half reclining on Kirk's knees, was watching him with such eager eyes.

"Let me—" and now Leo was doing something, unscrewing the cap of that tiny bottle.

Cold fluid hit sensitive skin, and Kirk gasped.

"Sorry," Leo said, shifting forward again, his weight on Kirk's thighs. He was intent, focused only on Kirk's arousal, and on his fingers pumping slowly up and down Kirk's shaft.

More slick fluid spilled onto his hand, and Kirk began to shudder.

"I won't—" he began, then gasped for breath. "Won't last—very long—if you—"

"If I what?" Leo said, like the horrible, terrible tease he was. "If I keep sitting on your lap? Or if I keep doing—this?" As his fingers tightened around Kirk's shaft, he gave a sinful little wriggle.

Kirk moaned.

"Do you want something else, then?" Leo asked as if he had no idea what that could be. "I could suck you off. We haven't done that in a while. Or, hmm, what *else* haven't we done in a while, I wonder…"

His voice trailed off, and he gave Kirk a shrewd, calculating look from under his eyelashes.

That shouldn't be so damn sexy, Kirk thought indignantly, but somehow everything Leo did exuded sex.

Now, Leo slid even closer, pressing himself against Kirk, sliding his erection against Kirk's until they were both shaking with the stimulation. One of Leo's hands slid under himself, he leaned back, and then Kirk realized with a sudden shock of lust that Leo was *preparing* himself. His fingers were slick and wet, and he was moaning softly, his bottom lip caught between his teeth.

When Leo looked up at him again, his eyes were a little hazy, his pupils wide and dark.

Kirk felt himself falling into those eyes.

His resistance crumbled, and he sealed Leo's lush, kiss-swollen mouth with his own.

Then he slid his big hands under Leo's thighs, lifting him up.

Leo moaned and wrapped his arms around Kirk's neck. "Yes," he said huskily, "yes, do it, do it—"

He was babbling, and Kirk stopped listening for words, paying more attention to the breathy sounds Leo made as Kirk lifted him up and positioned him until Kirk's cock was pressing right against his slick little opening.

For a long, breathless moment, Kirk held him there, enjoying Leo's moans of frustration.

"Payback for teasing me," he whispered in Leo's ear, and Leo laughed a little hoarsely.

"You are an awful, evil man, and if you don't start—oh god—" Leo's eyes widened as he felt Kirk begin to push into him. "Oh fuck, oh, you are so—"

Kirk felt sweat break out on his forehead as he tried desperately to go slow, to give Leo a little time to adjust to his bulk. He was only barely in, and the urge to *thrust* and *take* was overwhelming.

The slickness helped, but he could still feel Leo clamped tight around him, the muscle trying to resist, to push him out. He was so tight, clinging like velvet, and Kirk shook with the need to claim him again.

"You're mine," he said, a ritual declaration that he couldn't help making.

It felt so good to say it. So right.

"Yours," Leo affirmed instantly, breathing harshly into Kirk's ear as Kirk let him sink just a little more, let himself push up just a little more, opening him. "Oh, oh—"

They shook in each other's arms, the

chair creaking under their combined weight.

Leo bent forward and rested his forehead against Kirk's collarbone, breathing in great panting gasps.

Kirk's arms trembled. It wasn't the weight—it was the sheer effort of going slow, of maintaining control.

I won't hurt him. Never, ever.

"Do it," Leo whispered again, shivering, and he rolled his hips in a tight little circle that made Kirk see stars.

"You're not ready," Kirk rejoined, his voice sounding as rough as the tide over gravel.

"*Fuck* ready," Leo said urgently. He lifted up his head and pressed his lips against Kirk's, with an eager, ruthless fervor that Kirk couldn't possibly resist.

Then Leo pulled away, fixing Kirk with a challenging stare that awoke every primal instinct Kirk had.

"*Fuck me*," Leo demanded. He rolled his hips again, urgently.

With that, Kirk lost the remainder of his

control.

He growled, low in his throat, and pushed Leo down onto his cock.

Leo groaned, a long drawn-out sound that spiralled higher, and he nearly tipped over with the force of Kirk's thrust.

"You, oh—" Leo breathed, his voice shaky, "god, you don't know what it feels like— you're so big inside me—" his voice trailed off, and Kirk felt his breathing stutter.

Kirk ground into him, his hands clamped around Leo's slim waist, forcing him down onto the ramrod bulk of his cock.

He couldn't stop, he couldn't slow down, not anymore. Leo had woken the wolf in him, and there was no stopping now. There was only heat and lust and sheer animal *need*.

And Leo was urging him on with every breathless whimper, with every thud of his fists on Kirk's back. "Yes—do it—" he kept saying.

Sweat ran down Kirk's neck, and Leo's naked back was slippery with it, making it harder to hold on to him. But Kirk would never let go. He pushed hard, feeling the resistance slowly lessen. Leo was opening to him.

He thrust up hard, forcing Leo down. Then he took Leo's mouth as he fucked him, thrusting his tongue inside in the same rhythm. Leo's little cries and moans were swallowed up, and the only sound was the loud creaking of the chair and their harsh breathing.

Leo held on, even as Kirk plundered him ruthlessly, fucking him open with mindless brutal fervor. Leo sucked eagerly at Kirk's tongue, then let his head drop back so Kirk could see the long, beautiful, supple line of his throat.

That sight went to Kirk's head like a bolt of lightning.

He's submitting to me.

He's mine.

He's mine.

The wolf roared inside him, and suddenly having Leo sitting on top of him, riding out his thrusts, wasn't enough anymore. He needed more leverage. He needed to be deeper, deep inside Leo, owning him.

With a grunt, Kirk stood up, holding Leo tightly. His cock inevitably slipped out as he stood up, and Leo gave a long, complaining groan. "No—why—"

Kirk kicked the chair out of the way and put Leo down onto the kitchen table.

Leo blinked up at him, looking a little dazed. His legs were splayed wide open, dangling off the wooden edge of the table.

"Raise your legs," Kirk said, rough and low. "Hold yourself open for me."

He watched the way Leo's stomach muscles tightened as Leo tried to obey Kirk's orders, wriggling around on the table until he'd managed to grip his knees.

Then Leo lay back, his head hitting the table with a soft thud. His hands gripped tightly, holding his knees against his chest. He was so limber that it didn't even seem to be causing him any difficulty. And his eyes...his eyes weren't dazed now, they were blazing with need.

Kirk's breath caught at the vision in front of him.

Leo was wide open for him, wanting him.

He looked utterly wanton. Stretched and slippery and *hungry*. Waiting for him.

With a low growl, Kirk moved closer and took hold of Leo's waist again.

The height was just right. He could effortlessly slide into Leo, all the way in one long, long, utterly satisfying thrust, until his balls slapped against Leo's ass.

Leo moaned again, high and thin. His pupils were wide and black, almost obscuring the gorgeous blue of his eyes. Clouds of pheromones rose off him like steam, and he was rock hard, his cock almost up against his stomach in a fierce, needy curve.

"Yes," Leo whispered almost voicelessly. "Oh god, yes—please—do it to me—"

His fingers scrabbled against the table, as if looking for something to hold on to. But the table was too wide for him to grasp the edge, and he clenched his fists instead, nails digging into his palms.

Kirk slid halfway out, then pounded into him again with long hard thrusts, taking him ruthlessly.

He could feel the need rising inside him, spiraling up out of control, coiling around his spine like a tsunami of lust.

He was a mindless being, nothing but need and want, a creature of force and flame.

But Leo met his every thrust, raising up his hips a little, clamping down on him. And Leo's cries urged him on, higher, deeper, faster, harder—

—until the need became *now*.

He held Leo tight against him, hands clamped around his hips. With one more long satisfying thrust, he felt that need spill up and over and *out*, deep inside Leo, spilling into his warm, clinging body.

Kirk groaned. Utter satisfaction swept through him at the feeling of connection, of possession.

Leo was *his*.

Kirk's seed was deep inside him, Kirk's scent was all over him. There could be no question, no other claim. No other would ever have him like this.

He blinked sweat out of his eyes, feeling dazed. Little aftershocks shuddered through him.

When he looked down, trying to focus, Leo looked back up at him with a peculiar expression—half triumphant, half embarrassed.

Leo's stomach was spattered with white fluid, and his cock was limp against his stomach.

Kirk smiled slowly, realizing what had happened.

He had intended to take Leo into his mouth, suck him off with all the skill he could command—but it looked like events had passed him by.

Leo had come just from this, just from having Kirk's cock inside him. That sent a jolt of pride through Kirk.

"Sorry," Leo said huskily. "I—it was—you felt so good, I couldn't wait—"

"Don't apologize," Kirk said, his own voice as raw as if he'd been screaming.

Words failed him—words always failed

him in a moment like this—so he stroked Leo's cheek, as gently as he could, and Leo's eyes fluttered closed. He leaned into Kirk's touch, sighing.

Kirk's spent cock gave a twitch inside Leo, and Leo moaned.

"Relax," Kirk said. "Just—let me—"

As slowly as possible, Kirk withdrew, feeling Leo's slick flesh cling to him.

Leo moaned a little more, his tender muscle fluttering around Kirk's cock.

Kirk sighed when he finally slipped free. He didn't want to lose the connection between them.

But Leo smiled at him, a warm golden smile, and Kirk knew that the connection wasn't lost.

Bending close, Kirk gathered Leo up in his arms.

"Come on, sweetheart," he whispered, hardly aware of what he was saying. "Let's get you to bed."

***

When Leo woke, he was alone. Kicking off the mussed sheets, he slowly rolled out of bed, stretching and yawning.

"Kirk?" he called as he pulled on a fresh pair of boxer shorts, his voice hoarse with sleep.

There was no answer.

Leo wandered into the living room, then into the kitchen. There was no one there, but there were signs of a hurried breakfast: some crumbs on the kitchen table, a plate on the drying rack.

Then he saw the note, taped to a kitchen chair.

"Didn't want to wake you," it read, in a thick uneven script that made Leo's lip twitch into a fond smile. "Got a call to fix a roof near Silver Springs. Talk to the pack while I'm there."

And then, underlined twice: "Don't worry." And a tapering, curly scrawl that must be Kirk's name, not that Leo could even decipher it.

Leo shook his head. *Don't worry. Right.*

Then a thought hit his half asleep, fuzzy brain that shocked him into wakefulness.

It's Saturday.

He'd promised to help out at the art store. If things worked out, this was the start of his new job.

Damn it, Kirk, why didn't you wake me?

Leo had a feeling he knew why. It wasn't about the job; Kirk knew he had a job interview today, but not that it was early.

Leo should have set an alarm. But last night—he smiled to himself, remembering how wild they'd gotten—there had been no part of him that didn't want to just collapse into bed, and he'd forgotten all about it.

No, the real reason had to be that Kirk just loved watching him sleep.

Several times, Leo had come out of a half-dreaming state to find himself wrapped in Kirk's arms, Kirk's dark eyes watching him.

Maybe it should have felt strange, stifling even, but it didn't. It felt comforting.

Kirk always smiled a little when he saw Leo wake up, and then bent to kiss the tip of his nose before giving him his first real kiss of the day.

He missed that, today; he missed that warmth, that wonderful feeling of being safe and cherished and loved.

But I'll make up for it tonight, he promised himself.

He had to hurry. Kirk had taken the truck, but if Leo hustled, he could make it down to the main highway in time for the bus into town. A good thing that he'd stopped to figure out the timetable a day or so earlier; the bus only came by once an hour.

Breakfast would have to be on the go, this morning.

***

The bell clanged when Leo walked into the art store.

Mr Wilkins hobbled right into his path, smiling broadly. "Leo! Do you want to help me get started on unpacking these paints?"

It was as if he'd worked there for years.

"Be glad to," Leo said with a smile.

There were no customers, though the store was officially open. As they worked, unpacking boxes and crates and settling the contents in their rightful places on the shelves, Mr Wilkins told him what to expect.

"We open at 10 on Saturdays, but mostly people don't start coming in until 11. So we have an hour to get ready. If there's a lot of stock, I like to get started at 9. That suit you?"

Leo nodded. He slit open a big carton full of sketchbooks and began putting them away. The store was well organized, if a little cluttered, but his fingers ached to do some work on the dusty display in the window. He would save that possibility for later, though, when he knew just how much innovation Mr Wilkins could tolerate.

"So, your boyfriend doesn't mind you working on Saturdays?" Mr Wilkins asked, his sharp grey eyes raking Leo from head to foot.

Leo blinked, then dropped an armful of sketchbooks on the shelf with a thud. "He's working too."

For a moment, he stood stock still, trying to work out how he was going to handle this. He didn't know how *out* Kirk wanted to be...but this was a small town, where people paid attention to their neighbors.

And he kissed me in the middle of the parking lot.

It would be hard to hide something like this. And Leo didn't like lying, either.

He settled on compromise. "I never said Kirk was my boyfriend."

Mr Wilkins laughed his dry, dusty laugh. "Didn't have to. You start blushing as soon as anyone mentions him, for one thing. And if delicacy permitted me, I would add that you have that newlywed glow about you."

Leo sighed, feeling the heat rise in his cheeks. "Fine. Can we just...change the subject?"

Mr Wilkins handed him a jar full of pencils. "Here, go sort these according to hardness." His voice trailed off and he gave Leo a perfectly wicked little wink. "Maybe that's not enough of a subject change, huh?"

Leo laughed, surprised and a little shocked. "Mr Wilkins!" he protested.

"I may be old," Mr Wilkins said tartly, "but I'm not dead."

"No kidding." Leo started sorting the pencils, bending his head over his work. The blush wasn't going away any time soon.

"Hey," Mr Wilkins said, and his sharp voice was just a little softer now. "Don't worry. I like a joke, but I'm not going to harass you. It's just nice to see some young love around here. Brightens everything up, like spring."

Leo felt a rush of affection for the old man. "It's okay," he said, "just—I'm still getting used to it, myself."

"Ah," Mr Wilkins said, nodding. Then his eyes began to twinkle again. "I'm sure you'll have him broken in soon enough."

Leo chuckled and didn't reply, since Mr Wilkins was obviously determined to have the last word. But he was warmed by the old man's easy acceptance.

They kept working, and soon all the boxes and crates were empty and the store was fully restocked.

Leo began breaking up the cardboard boxes, stacking them for recycling, while Mr Wilkins swept the floor.

"Well, that certainly went faster than usual," Mr Wilkins said at last, leaning on his broom and looking satisfied. "Still early. Time for a cup of tea, don't you think?"

Leo had a suspicion that Mr Wilkins practically lived on tea. In the tiny kitchen— more like a closet—that belonged to the store's back room, he had a whole cupboard devoted to various teas: green, black, herbal, all in different tins and boxes, some of them labeled only in Japanese.

Leo watched as he made the tea,

admiring the deft precision of his movements.

Carrying two cups of steaming, fragrant jasmine tea, they sat down behind the counter together.

"Here's what I can offer you," Mr Wilkins said, shoving a piece of paper toward him. There were some figures scrawled on it. "It's not a full week, can't afford that. Thursdays, Fridays and Saturdays are the busiest, so that's when I could use you. See what you think."

Leo read the figures and raised his eyebrows. It was more than he had expected.

Mr Wilkins watched him shrewdly. "Good offer?"

Leo nodded slowly. Maybe he ought to haggle, but it didn't really feel right. After unpacking the stock and pricing the items, it was easy enough to see that the store's margins were thin, and the salary was fair. "Yeah. I'll take it."

"Good. I knew you were a smart city boy, so I gave you my final offer right off. Saves time."

Leo laughed. "Thanks. I didn't expect

that."

Mr Wilkins tilted his head, looking like a bright-eyed little bird. "Kirk tell you I'd be trouble?"

"...kind of." Leo took a sip of tea, smiling.

"Well, takes one to know one," Mr Wilkins said philosophically. "His father was the most ornery man who ever lived. Full of pride and without the sense God gave a sparrow. At least Kirk got his mother's brains, I'll say that for him."

Leo swallowed the tea hurriedly. It felt like a window was suddenly opening into Kirk's past, and he couldn't stop himself from wanting to know more. "You knew his parents?"

"Course I did," Mr Wilkins said complacently. "This is Sevenacres, everyone knows everyone. And his mother Marilee...ah, she was a beauty. Long dark hair, green eyes—you'd stop on the sidewalk just to look at her. When she married John Anderson, she broke hearts all over town."

Leo wasn't surprised. Kirk's mesmerizing looks had to come from somewhere. Though Kirk didn't have green eyes—at least, not until full moon.

For a moment, Leo lost track of what Mr Wilkins was saying. His mind was full of Kirk's glowing eyes, unearthly and strange, fixed on Leo with an intent, hungry expression. That was how Kirk had looked during the claiming—more wolf than man, for all that he was wearing his human skin.

Just the memory of that look was enough to send a bolt of desire through Leo.

He blinked, trying to focus on his surroundings, and on the sharp, dry voice of Mr Wilkins.

"And we didn't see him for years, after his parents died in that crash—"

With a shock, Leo realized that Mr Wilkins was now talking about Kirk.

"They died in a crash?" he interrupted, feeling his heart seize with sudden grief for Kirk. He hadn't wanted to ask, but he knew that Kirk must have lost both his parents when he was still pretty young, given the way he talked about them. Leo just hadn't known that it was so sudden and brutal.

Mr Wilkins nodded, his bristly brows lowering. "It was appalling. John Anderson liked to drive fast—mind you, I'm not saying that the accident was his fault, don't go repeating that to his son—and we all knew him to get a speeding ticket now and then. But then, one night, he must've lost control of the wheel and drove straight into Cedar Pass. Took forever to recover the bodies."

Leo swallowed, his mouth suddenly gone dry. "And Kirk?"

Mr Wilkins gave him a look of sympathy. "Kirk was on a high school trip, some hiking thing, camping out in the woods. The principal had to drive out and give him the news."

Leo closed his eyes, trying to imagine Kirk as a teenager, out in the woods he loved so much. *It must have felt like his world had ended.*

Mr Wilkins said, "We were all glad to see Kirk come back, later, after he got out of the Army. He kept the cabin, but nobody lived in it since his parents died. And then one day, he was just suddenly there. Like he never left."

"Must have been a surprise," Leo said,

thinking about the day he'd met Kirk. That summed it up pretty well: *he was just suddenly there*. Like a freaking miracle, appearing just when Leo thought he was doomed to die out in the woods, alone.

"He didn't say why he came back. He's never been what you might call talkative," Mr Wilkins said.

Leo tried to suppress a snort of laughter. "I believe you."

"But after the Army, he really clammed up. Barely said a word to anyone. Didn't even go out drinking, as far as we could tell." Mr Wilkins darted a sudden, sharp look toward him. "But I've heard people say that recently, it's like someone turned on the light for him. He's a different man altogether."

Leo tried to hide his smile behind his cup of tea.

"That's what I thought," Mr Wilkins said, with a satisfied little cackle. "Now, look out the window—I can see Marie-Ann Jackson headed this way. You look alive and help her, she's going to want some new canvas, if I know my customers."

Leo jumped off his stool, glad to assist.

A heavyset, russet-haired woman walked in the door, smiling warmly as soon as she spotted Mr Wilkins. "Morning, Henry. Finally got some help in, did ya?"

"About time," Henry agreed. "Marie-Ann, this is Leo. Lives up at Kirk's place, you know."

"Oh, yeah?" Marie-Ann said, with another lovely smile for Leo. "Hiya, Leo. Can you help me find some linen canvas?"

"Nice to meet you," Leo said. "Pre-stretched linen canvas, or raw? And what sizes are you looking for?"

"Oh, always raw, I prefer to stretch them myself," Marie-Ann said, smiling.

Leo nodded, biting his bottom lip to prevent a chuckle from escaping. It was Mr Wilkins's fault, he thought, that everything these people said now sounded like innuendo to his ears. "I'll find you some stretcher bars, too."

"I like him, Henry," Marie-Ann called past Leo's shoulder. "Knows his stuff. I thought you just hired him for his pretty face."

Mr Wilkins chuckled. "Who says I can't do both?"

More customers walked in, which was a useful distraction, because Leo was fighting another blush and trying hard to appear as professional as possible.

His new job certainly promised to be... interesting.

***

Kirk drove into Silver Springs feeling strangely unsettled. It was almost as though a physical tie existed between Leo and himself: some kind of high-tension wire that stretched and stretched the further he drove away from his home. It felt uncomfortable to be out of reach, out of hearing.

What was Leo doing, right now? Was he cooking a leisurely breakfast, wearing those old sweatpants that barely clung to his hips? Was he out on the porch, finishing his painting of the yellow-leaved birches?

Or was he still asleep, curled up around a pillow as if he feared Kirk would steal it from him?

That was how Leo had looked when Kirk left. Asleep, his long lashes spiky on his cheek, his blond hair mussed, with a pillow in his arms and another under his head.

Kirk's lips curved into a private smile. He envied that pillow.

Focus, he told himself. He couldn't be mooning over Leo when he met up with the wolf pack, the Reds. For one thing, they would smell it on him. And his distraction might give them some kind of advantage.

Silver Springs was a beautiful town, a little smaller than Sevenacres. It was quieter, and the people who lived here were, on the whole, richer. It showed in the cars they drove, the carefully manicured lawns, and the boutique shops along the main street.

Kirk felt a little out of place in his old truck, wearing his usual combo of jeans, boots, and flannel shirt. Almost defiantly, he turned the radio up louder. It was tuned to a rock station he could only tolerate half the month:

the wolf had sensitive hearing, and the loud monotony of rock beats didn't sound so good on the days around the full moon.

But right now, he could nod his head and tap his foot to the beat of an old Creedence song, though he wasn't going to try to sing along. He'd leave that to Leo, who seemed to sing as unselfconsciously as he did...well...just about everything else.

That was one of the amazing things about Leo. He didn't need to hold up a mask to the world, the way most people did. Whatever he felt was visible on his face, in his body language, and in the heady fragrance of his scent. And if there was any doubt, he would be quick enough to put those feelings into words.

It was a facility that Kirk lacked, and he knew it. All his life, people had told him that he was hard to read. And behind his back, with the uncomfortably sharp hearing the change bestowed on him, he heard other things. That he was proud, shy, morose; a misanthrope; a hermit.

Apparently it never occurred to those people that expressing your feelings, or making easy conversation, were skills just like any other. Skills that Kirk had never had any talent for.

But he had to admit that after he'd been turned into—no, not a monster; Leo would frown at him if he knew that Kirk still thought of himself that way—a werewolf, he had little desire to improve those skills, anyway.

What was the point of talking to people, when he couldn't even give an honest answer to some of the questions that came up in casual conversation?

Kirk snorted, thinking of some of the answers he could give.

Do you like hunting? — Yes, but only with my teeth and claws. Using guns is cheating.

Wasn't that a lovely harvest moon last night? — Yes, I spent several hours howling at it.

I lost my dog. Did you see her anywhere? — Yes, she's in heat and I can smell her from miles away. Don't worry, she'll come back when she's exhausted all the local strays.

Kirk had a feeling none of those would go

over well.

His truck rattled as he took the curve into the main square of Silver Springs. There was a small parking lot here, next to the church. It would be easier to sniff out the wolf pack on foot.

He didn't know their exact location. All he knew was that Brand, their leader, had agreed to stay here, outside Kirk's territory.

From what Brand had told him, the wolves had been looking for a place they could make their own. It wasn't Kirk's business how they did it; but he found that he was curious.

He still knew so little of what it was like to live in a pack like that. Hunting together, running together at the full moon, that he could understand. And he knew how good it could feel: an effortless sense of belonging that ran at the deepest levels, like family.

But what did the pack do during the rest of the month, when they were men? Did they hold down jobs, were they living together? It all seemed very strange. In Sevenacres, the Reds had been camping out, driving into town every day to eat at the diner. But that was more the way tourists behaved. They couldn't keep that up forever.

He parked the truck and stepped out, inhaling deeply.

The town smelled different, too. Like new cars, woodsmoke, and rich perfume.

There was a faint trace of wolf scent; not very prominent, several days old. Wherever the wolf pack was, it wasn't here in the town square.

Kirk began to walk, sniffing inobtrusively now and then.

Wherever they were, he would find them.

***

As it turned out, the werewolves were working the upper slopes of Silver Springs, the most affluent part of town. Here, the houses were more like mansions, each overlooking the river valley far below.

Now Kirk *really* felt conspicuous.

Should have brought my toolbox, he

thought, walking up the driveway of *The Aspens*, a massive white wooden house that looked immaculately kept up. *At least then the people who live here would just write me off as the hired help, instead of a potential threat.* He noticed several curtains twitching from the neighboring house as he approached.

"Kirk!" said a loud, familiar voice as Kirk's boots crunched up the gravel driveway. "So glad you could come! How are you doing, how's Leo?"

Kirk's lips twitched. Brand sounded as if Kirk was doing him a favor by showing up here unexpectedly. That was typical of him. It put Kirk solidly in the position of *invited guest*, not *interloper*.

Brand was saying, *I know you're too smart to come here and threaten me, so let's pretend I asked you over.* And though it looked like Brand was meeting him alone, Kirk could smell several other werewolves nearby, ready and waiting. Just in case.

"We're good," Kirk said shortly. He felt uncomfortable, standing here in the driveway of a mansion whose owners he'd never met, and no doubt that was deliberate, too. "You work here?"

"Indeed," Brand said, his rich voice lingering on the word. "Come in, there's nobody home."

They walked up to the back door, which led into a kitchen. Not the main kitchen, clearly; there was no gleaming chrome, just simple, functional appliances. The servants' kitchen.

As they walked in, Kirk looked Brand up and down. The pack leader was wearing all black, with a fitted vest that looked somehow strange, too heavily padded to flatter the bulk of Brand's body. Kirk sniffed at it and caught a strange scent: silicon, ceramics. *Ah. Bulletproof.*

"Yes," Brand answered his unspoken thought. "We signed on as private security. A special taskforce. There's been a rash of burglaries lately."

Kirk thought about that for a second. He had a strong suspicion that Brand's sense of morality was dubious, at best. "Before or after you guys came into town?"

Brand grinned, baring strong canines. "You're quick, Kirk. I like that about you."

Kirk shook his head, though he couldn't

help smiling a little. He didn't approve of the way the wolf pack treated normal humans: like toys, like things to be pushed around. But a part of him had to admire the sheer audacity of what they were doing.

Brand sniffed back at him companionably, a wolf's greeting. "Mm, Leo's doing well, I see. And—" he paused, and his affable expression changed into something a little darker, though it quickly smoothed over again.

Kirk nodded back grimly. There was an advantage to dealing with another werewolf; some things didn't need to be spelled out. "Yes. Erick."

Brand shook his head. "He came up to the cabin?"

"No, he harassed Leo in town. *My* town. I wasn't there."

"Of course," Brand muttered. "He's afraid of you."

"But not afraid to make trouble, apparently."

Brand turned his head and spoke into the

tiny, barely visible mike that was clipped to the collar of his dark jacket. "Mike, Stepan, Jason. Come over to the house."

Within a minute, the kitchen was full of werewolves. All of them were dressed like Brand, with black jackets that said '*Reds Home Safety*' on the back.

"Erick broke the truce," Brand told them simply. "We deal with this *now*. Pack rules."

Stepan was the oldest, a tall, spare man with grizzled hair. He nodded to Brand, then to Kirk. "We'll find him." His eyes were cold.

Kirk nodded back, sizing up the trio.

He had a feeling Brand had picked these men for a reason. They weren't like the two werewolves he had seen Erick with, the ones who had accompanied him when he brought Leo to the clearing on the full moon. These men were older, and they looked like they would be loyal to Brand, not to Erick.

"Bring Erick to the house," Brand ordered. "I'll meet you there. Get Jack, Buzz, and Derek to take over guard duty here."

House? Kirk lifted his eyebrows as the

three men left to obey Brand's orders.

Brand nodded. "Yeah, we're not camping out anymore. We rented a place up on the east slopes. It's usually empty until the skiing season, so they gave us a discount."

"And you all live there," Kirk said dubiously. He couldn't imagine what that was like. An entire wolf pack, all crammed into one house? That sounded like a nightmare.

Brand laughed, a rich warm sound. "Wait until you see it."

***

Kirk drove up the long winding road behind Brand's motorcycle, wondering if he'd lost his mind.

Here he was dealing with the wolf pack *again*, when the whole point of the truce had been to keep them away from him until the full moon.

He didn't want to be here. He wanted to be home, waiting for Leo to come home from work.

Then he had to laugh at himself. *How domestic can you get?*

Still, it was true. Ever since his transformation, he'd longed for companionship, for people who would understand what had been done to him. He hadn't even dared dream about the existence of other werewolves.

But now that he knew other werewolves existed, now that he even had the option to join them and live with them, perhaps even lead them...now, he didn't need that anymore. To run with the wolves at full moon, yes—that was a priceless gift he wouldn't soon give up—but not to share his life with them on the other days of the month.

What he needed was to be with the one who had claimed his heart.

To share his life with Leo.

Kirk set his jaw, determined to open the topic with Leo soon.

Tonight, if possible.

It was a risk. If Leo wasn't ready for

commitment, Kirk could end up driving him away.

But in his heart, he hoped that Leo was ready. Leo had made several huge commitments already: he'd gone through the claiming ritual of the wolf pack for Kirk's sake, and he'd found himself a job in Sevenacres. That didn't sound like he was planning to leave any time soon.

It was just difficult to believe, that was all.

Kirk wasn't used to having his dreams come true. All he knew was what it was like to be alone.

Ahead, Brand took the last curve with a flourish, sending sprays of gravel into the bushes by the side of the road, and stopped in a parking lot where several motorcycles were already parked.

Kirk parked his truck next to Brand's motorcycle, just under the sign that said: *Private Parking, Ridge House only.* Then he looked up, past the rhododendron bushes that bordered the parking lot, and his breath caught.

Above him, set dramatically on top of a hill, a huge wooden post-and-beam mansion towered. It wasn't anything like what he had envisioned: some sort of simple wooden bunkhouse where all the werewolves camped together, with bunk beds in unwelcome proximity.

This looked almost like a castle. There was even a tower, jutting out from the left side, with huge windows overlooking the valley.

"It's quite a place," Brand said, following his gaze. "Ten bedrooms, ten bathrooms. And there's a hot tub in the tower." He met Kirk's astonished eyes with a broad smile, and his scent changed, becoming richer, muskier. "Want to try it out?"

Kirk shook his head, accustomed to this form of persuasion by now. Brand seemed to lead through sex as much as through dominance, but Kirk wasn't a full member of his pack, and he owed Brand no sexual allegiance.

Brand was an attractive man, and a striking wolf—big, muscular, generously endowed—but Kirk wasn't even tempted. All he had room for in his life was Leo.

Brand took the rebuff with easy grace. "Come and have a look around, then. We need to talk about Erick before the others get here."

***

Leo shook out his shoulders, trying to ease the tension there. As fun as his first work day at the art store had been, he felt exhausted now that it was over. And it was a long walk back up from the bus stop to Kirk's cabin.

As he trudged up the last curve in the road, he found himself thinking fondly of a hot bath. A long, hot, muscle-melting bath, and then a late supper. Oh man, that sounded *so* good.

Was Kirk home already?

Leo craned his neck, but he didn't see the truck anywhere. And there was no light in any of the windows.

A wave of disappointment washed over him. He was simply, purely, longing for Kirk; he wanted to walk in the door and melt straight into his arms.

No complications. No conversations.

Just walk into his arms and feel them wrap around me, so warm...and then a kiss, that strong mouth on mine...

He sighed. The mental image was so convincing that it was heart-wrenching to let go of it and accept that he would have to wait.

Don't be so dramatic, he told himself. *I'm sure he'll be home soon.*

Through drifts of fallen leaves, he walked up to the front door. There was no key to search for; Kirk had told him nobody here ever locked their doors. Leo was still trying to get used to that idea. He was too much of a city boy to take security for granted.

He pushed open the screen door and went inside. Left his boots in the hallway under the bench, wandered into the bathroom to start a bath, and then into Kirk's bedroom to undress —

— where he got the shock of his life.

There was someone sitting on the bed, a dark shape against the bright white curtains.

It wasn't Kirk.

"Jesus, Mary and Joseph," Leo yelled, reeling back against the door. His heart hammered in his chest, and he could feel his pulse jumping.

Erick smiled at him, stretched as slowly and languidly as a cat, and rolled off the bed. His motorcycle leathers were spread out on the bed, and he was wearing a soft white sweater and jeans. "What a quaint expression," he said pensively. "I didn't know you were a Catholic."

Leo couldn't answer him. He was too busy almost having a heart attack. There were dark spots in front of his eyes, and he shook his head to get rid of them, feeling more than a little woozy.

Slowly, his sense of balance returned.

Erick was slowly moving toward him, with a predatory gleam in his eyes.

"What are you doing here?" Leo sputtered. He scrabbled behind him to get the door open. "I'm calling the police."

"Don't be silly, I'd just tell them you invited me here for sex," Erick said calmly. "And you did. Didn't you? You even kept my gift, just like I thought you would."

He waved something in his hand, and Leo recognized the heavy object Erick had slipped into his jacket pocket days ago.

I knew I should have thrown that out, he thought, with a stab of annoyance at himself.

It was just...difficult to do. The object was a *netsuke*, a solid ivory sculpture the size of a walnut, carved in the shape of a dragon biting into its own tail. It was an antique, hand-carved by an artist long ago, beautiful and irreplacable. Not the sort of thing Leo could just throw into the thrash.

Reluctantly, he'd put it on a shelf in the living room, waiting for the right moment to tell Kirk about it and figure out what to do with it.

Leo shook his head again, trying to focus.

Erick was standing close to him. He'd turned on the overhead lights in the bedroom. The light shone on the white dragon, making it gleam in Erick's pale hand.

"You smell so intoxicating," Erick said softly. "Do you have any idea how irresistible you are? Do you even know how Kirk found you, that day in the woods? It wasn't an accident."

Leo watched the way the dragon rolled back and forth in Erick's hand.

It was difficult to think, and his anger slowly turned to confusion.

What was Erick *doing* to him? What was he talking about?

"Kirk followed your scent to find you," Erick told him, smiling faintly. "It's not love, dear Leo. It's pure pheromones that brought you two together. The chemistry of sex, and the enormous appetite of wolves. Kirk's out with the pack right now, isn't he? What do you think they're doing?"

Leo tried to think, biting down hard on his upper lip to bring back some focus to his scattered thoughts. But even the small stab of pain seemed fuzzy and far away. "Talking," he said hazily. "About—uh—"

"That's what Kirk told you, isn't it," Erick said, shaking his head with a look of scornful pity. "No, darling. They're not *talking*. You just don't realize what it's like to be a werewolf. Our appetites are beyond what any human can take. And he doesn't trust himself with you. He thinks you're fragile, too easily hurt. So now that he's found some of his own people, who *can* take what he dishes out—"

Leo clenched his fists. "You're wrong. He wouldn't do that."

Dimly, he was aware that his reality was shifting, melting. The shadows on the wall seemed to grow longer, the overhead light brighter, and the carved dragon in Erick's hand became almost blindingly white. He couldn't take his eyes away from it.

"Forget Kirk," Erick was saying. "Think of yourself for a change. Think of what you're worth, what you could be. You're an artist. You should live surrounded by beauty, instead of in this hovel. Do you like the dragon? I bought it just for you."

Leo watched it sway back and forth in Erick's hand. It was becoming harder and harder to think clearly.

"Yes," he said hazily. The dragon was beautifully carved, every tiny scale, every minute claw. It was a work of art. How could he *not* like it?

"Oh, good. I like hearing you say yes to me," Erick said softly, his voice curling around

Leo so gently, so insistently. "I want to hear you say yes again, and again, and again. In bed and out of it."

He was standing very close now, his long pale hand holding the dragon in front of Leo's eyes.

His other arm was around Leo's shoulders, curving around him.

How had *that* happened?

Leo blinked, confused. It was hard to focus on anything but the dragon, so gleaming and white, so small, so perfect.

Erick bent close and took a long, deep breath, inhaling. Taking in his scent.

"God, you're gorgeous," Erick breathed. His long blond hair fell forward, tickling Leo's shoulder. It had a subtle flowery scent to it, like jasmine. "Say yes to me again, dearest."

"Go 'way," Leo said, trying to push the words out through the thick layer of cotton that had wrapped itself around his tongue. As he spoke, he swayed on his feet, but Erick caught him and steadied him.

"Easy," Erick said. "You're very susceptible, aren't you." There was a note of amused satisfaction in his voice. "Susceptible, yet stubborn."

"'M not," Leo muttered.

Erick nuzzled his neck, licking at the warm spot under his jaw. "You're tired," he said softly, his voice sounding rougher, deeper. Familiar. "Let me take care of you. Let me take you to bed. It's been a long day."

Leo tried to keep to his feet, but the floor was melting under him. It was true. He *was* tired. And he wanted...he'd been longing for...

Erick was holding him up with surprising strength, bending close, his arm like a bar of steel around Leo's shoulders. His breath was warm upon Leo's cheek.

Leo only had to turn his head a little, just a little, to turn it into a kiss.

Erick's mouth was strong and warm, his lips velvet-soft, and for a moment, Leo forgot everything.

***

Kirk walked up the broad wooden stairs behind Brand, hearing them creak under their combined weight. The stairs were the only access to the house on the hill, and he had no doubt that that was one reason why Brand had chosen this place for the pack. Ridge House was built high enough to have a view of the entire Silver Springs valley, and there was no way for anyone to approach unnoticed.

Brand slid a keycard into a slot, and the front door swung open. They walked in.

There was no doubt that the house was gorgeous. The long marble-floored hallway led into a large open space. It was a living room with enormously high ceiling rafters, big white sofas, and a fireplace large enough to roast a boar in. One wall was all glass, a giant window overlooking the valley, and Kirk was drawn to it immediately.

"Yeah, this is what sold me on this place," Brand was saying, looking smug.

The view was amazing, Kirk had to admit. The river wound into silver half-circles, surrounded by forest almost to the horizon. The access road was just out of view, hidden away to the right of the window. It looked as though the house was set in a wilderness, untouched by human hands.

And at night, you could watch the moon rise...

The thought made him a little envious. His cabin wasn't like this. It was cozy, and it felt like home to him, but it wasn't a dramatic backdrop to an overwhelming view.

Still, Leo seemed to like the birch trees near the cabin. And the bath, and the fireplace. And Kirk wanted to share his home only with Leo, not with a whole pack of werewolves.

Kirk watched a heron wing over the river, long legs arrow-straight behind its silver-grey body.

"Wine?" Brand asked him. He set down a tray of glasses and bottles on a table by one of the big white sofas. "Or something stronger?"

"Wine," Kirk said after a moment's thought. He wasn't much of a drinker, but one glass wouldn't hurt him. And he had a feeling Brand would have chosen something good. Brand was a hedonist, after all.

Brand poured red wine into two glasses and handed one to Kirk. "You'll like this," he said. "It's a Ventoux from Chateau Pesquié. Not a wine most people have heard of—"

Certainly not me, Kirk thought. What he knew about wine could be summed up in very few sentences. *It's white or red and made from grapes,* that about covered it.

As Brand talked on about micro-climates in the Valley of the Rhone and *grenache* and *syrah* grapes, Kirk tasted his wine.

It was excellent, there was no doubt about that. The heady, fruity aroma made him want to stick his nose into the glass and somehow absorb the scent into his skin.

Brand watched him, grinning. "Good, huh? I worked as a wine importer for a while, picked up some tricks. Just another way in which our gift can benefit us."

Our *gift*. Kirk frowned. He still couldn't think of being a werewolf as a gift, as something like a talent—something that set him apart from others, that he was supposed to be proud of.

"It's not a gift to me," he said, trying to keep his voice civil. "I've always thought of it as a curse."

Brand shook his head. "I wish you'd had the benefit of knowing some other werewolves earlier on, Kirk. You need a fresh perspective on this." He paused, rolling the wine around in his glass before taking a sip, then sighed appreciatively. "Almost everyone in this pack was made, not born. They *wanted* the change."

Kirk shook his head. "Why would anyone want this?"

"They wanted to be strong," Brand told him in that rich, reasonable-sounding voice. "Some of them were sick. Buzz—you've seen him, the fast talker with the ginger hair—he had leukemia."

Kirk blinked. This wasn't something he'd heard about before. "And now?"

"Now he doesn't, of course. Werewolves don't *get* sick. Our blood is too strong. You knew that, didn't you?"

Kirk took a hasty swallow of wine, barely

tasting it as it went down. "I...wasn't sure."

More and more, it was becoming clear to him that he knew *nothing* about werewolves. All he knew was his own experience, which was unique. And not something he could tell Brand about. It would feel like betrayal, if he told Brand about something so intimate before telling Leo.

"And some of the others...once they knew what it was like for us—the freedom, the company of your fellow wolves, running together under the stars—they wanted it, too. They *chose* it. I'm getting the feeling you weren't given a choice."

Kirk turned away from Brand's far too knowing eyes. He faced the window again and stared out over the valley without seeing it. This wasn't something he wanted to discuss, not here, not now.

"Oh, and before the others get back here, I should tell you about Erick," Brand said.

His voice sounded casual—*too* casual, Kirk thought. His hackles rose. "What about him?"

Brand lifted the glass of wine up to the

light, as if inspecting its rich red color for flaws. "He was born, not made. One of the few. His parents were werewolves, too."

Kirk tried to imagine that. A werewolf family. It sounded...grotesque.

"It's very unusual for that to happen," Brand went on. "If it wasn't, there would be more werewolves than people. But for some reason, female werewolves are incredibly rare." He took a long, slow drink of wine. "When women get bitten, they don't change into werewolves; they just die. Happens to men, too, but more to women."

Kirk nodded, trying to absorb this new information as best as possible. It made his head spin. "So, why are you telling me this? What does it matter that Erick was born a werewolf?"

For all that Brand loved to talk, Kirk could tell that this was no trivial conversation. Brand was trying to warn him about something, in his own roundabout way.

"Sometimes, a born werewolf has—a little extra," Brand said carefully. "A gift that other werewolves don't have. He's stronger than the

rest, or can see in the dark better, or...
something else."

"Erick isn't stronger than us," Kirk said.
He felt utterly sure of that fact. Even though, as
much as he would like to fight Erick, he hadn't
yet done so. If Erick was that strong, he would
already be leading the pack. He was no match
even for Brand, let alone Kirk.

"No, you're right," Brand admitted. "But
Erick has a gift that's a little harder to
determine. Some of the younger wolves call him
a shaman."

"Why?"

"His voice," Brand said. "If you're not
vulnerable to it, it's hard to explain. But he can
be incredibly persuasive. It's a little like
hypnosis, I guess."

"And it works on werewolves?" Kirk
asked, dubious.

"It works on *some* werewolves. Mostly
the younger ones, the ones who aren't that
strong yet. They're easier to influence. But it
works *really* well on normal humans. The better
their imagination, the more receptive they are,
and the faster they go down. I've seen him

practically put someone under with his voice alone."

A memory struck Kirk with the force of a hammer blow.

Leo, looking lost, an expression that sat strangely on his expressive face.

Leo saying, *'He talked about—about—he took my car keys...'* in an uncertain, stammering voice that was completely unlike him.

"He used that trick on Leo," Kirk said, the words almost strangling in his throat.

Rage swept through him, boiling in his blood, threatening to erupt and overflow.

"Put the wine glass down," Brand said. Sharp, harsh words that cut through the red haze in Kirk's mind.

Kirk set the wine glass down on a side table with a ringing noise, one second before it would have splintered in his hand.

"Good. Now take it easy," Brand told him. "My boys are going after Erick. They'll find him. There's nothing to do but wait until they get back here."

Kirk shook his head. "I can't do that," he said grimly.

The wolf inside him was howling, *You left Leo alone. You* left *him. What if Erick's there with him, right* now?

He strode to the door, but Brand was suddenly in front of him, a hand on his shoulder. "Kirk. Listen. We need to deal with Erick according to pack rules. He broke the truce, he'll pay for it. But don't go off alone. Don't do anything stupid. You hear me?"

Kirk shook off the hand. "Leo's home alone," he growled at Brand. "If Erick's with him —your boys better hope they find him first."

Brand threw up his arms in exasperation, but he made no further attempt to stop Kirk.

"Just get him back here!" he yelled after Kirk as he strode down the hallway. "Get him back here and let the pack deal with him!"

"No promises," Kirk said.

***

Leo tore himself away from the kiss, breathing hard. He felt dizzy and sick, and Erick's arms were around him, holding him too close, too tight. "Let me go!"

For a moment, it had felt just like he was kissing Kirk. That deep, rough voice seemed to sink directly into his skin, warming him, reassuring him that everything was all right.

It wasn't until he felt Erick's smooth cheek against his own, instead of Kirk's heavy stubble, that he knew he was being tricked.

Erick looked down at him, surprise and displeasure clear in his face, before his expression smoothed out again. "Dear Leo, there's no need to be dramatic. Just listen to me —"

"No," Leo said, lifting his chin in defiance. That was the problem in the first place. He'd been listening to Erick, and he had no idea why.

When Erick didn't move, Leo huffed with irritation and stamped down on Erick's foot. *Hard.*

Leo was wearing hiking boots, but Erick had taken his motorcycle boots off along with the rest of his riding gear. The impact of Leo's heel crunching into Erick's sock-clad instep was incredibly satisfying.

"Ow!" Erick yelped, looking astonished and indignant. He hopped backwards, letting go of Leo to cradle his injured foot. "You son of a bitch!"

For all his anger, Leo couldn't resist the sudden laughter that bubbled up inside him. Erick hopping about on one foot, his long hair flying, was a ridiculous sight.

Whatever power Erick wielded over him seemed to be gone as soon as Leo laughed. His vision cleared; he felt like himself again.

"I don't want you here," Leo said pointedly. "Nobody wants you here. Leave, and take your stupid dragon with you."

Erick flushed. It was satisfying to see someone else at the mercy of their fair skin, Leo thought. Erick's cheeks were fiery with color, and his eyes glittered with anger and injured pride.

"Think again," Erick said softly. "There's no sense in staying with a solitary werewolf. What does he know? He's an outcast who doesn't know the meaning of love. Come with me and see what I have to offer you. We'll travel. See the world together."

For a moment, just a small fraction of time, Erick's words hung in the air like a soap bubble: fragile, beautiful, iridescent, glimmering with promise.

The seductive power in Erick's voice washed over Leo like a wave, filling him with longing. To see the world, to travel and see new things, beauty, art...find inspiration there...

He shook his head, dispelling the vision, and the soap bubble burst. "I'm staying here." He took a deep breath. "And you're not."

Erick's icy blue eyes raked him from head to toe. "You're a fool."

Just as Leo prepared to give a withering answer, the door to the bedroom swung open.

Kirk stood in the doorway, glowering.

***

The force of Kirk's glare could have melted steel.

"Out," Kirk growled, jerking his head at Erick.

Erick blinked. He met Kirk's angry eyes for one tense second, and then all the fight seemed to drain out of him. He left the room, limping.

To Leo's surprise, Kirk didn't tear after him. Instead, he stood in front of the bedroom door, arms folded in an impressive display of bulging muscle. He stared at Leo, fierce and intent and utterly unreadable.

Leo glared right back. "You took your sweet time getting here."

Kirk snorted. "Actually, I drove hell for leather, and you're welcome." He took a step forward, coming closer.

Leo stayed put. He lifted his chin, stubborn and sure of himself. After everything that had just happened, the last thing he needed was Kirk working out his anger on *him*.

"Did he hurt you?" Kirk growled.

Leo shook his head. Then, despite the tension, a grin quirked his lips. "Quite the reverse. Didn't you see him limp?"

Kirk blinked. He ground to a halt, looking as surprised as if Leo had just knocked him over. "I thought—his voice—"

"You could have warned me," Leo said. He folded his arms, watching Kirk's confusion with some satisfaction. "I didn't know his voice was so dangerous."

"Neither did I," Kirk said, still in that gravelly voice, and now he took one more step, bringing him into Leo's reach. "When Brand told me, I—" He sniffed the air, and his expression darkened.

"If you tell me I smell like him, *again*, I'm going to break something," Leo told him tartly. "I've had a really long day, and the last thing I need—"

Kirk unfolded his arms, and Leo's next words were muffled into his chest as Kirk pulled him close.

Then Kirk bent his head, and their mouths met.

It was nothing like Erick's kiss. It was overwhelming, a storm of want and need, and Leo lost himself in it.

Rough stubble scraped his cheek. Kirk's immensely powerful arms folded around him, and he knew himself to be safe, beloved, and wanted.

Leo sank into the kiss, tipping his head back. Kirk's mouth claimed his, strong but sweet, and for a while they spoke without words in the language they both knew best.

When they finally broke apart, Leo sighed with regret. "Don't stop," he pleaded, nuzzling Kirk's collarbone.

Kirk's eyes met his, dark with longing.

"We need to deal with Erick," Kirk said. Though he was still stroking Leo's cheek as if he couldn't tear himself away, either. "Once and for all. Will you come?"

"I thought you let him go, just now," Leo

said, confused.

He didn't want to talk about Erick. He just wanted Kirk to keep holding him like this, warm and safe.

Kirk shook his head. "There are three pack members on the porch. They're holding him for me." He smiled grimly. "It was that or break his neck."

Oh, Leo mouthed, feeling unsettled.

Rubbing at his stubbled jaw, Kirk added, "Don't think I wasn't tempted. But I prefer to stay on the right side of the law."

Leo didn't know how he felt about that. He was relieved that Kirk wasn't putting himself into danger. But all the same, he wished they were alone right now, instead of having werewolves nearby who could hear every word they said. He wished that they didn't have to deal with any of this. *I just want to be alone with you.*

Kirk nuzzled his neck, licking him. By now, Leo recognized that touch for what it was. He was erasing Erick's scent, overlaying it with his own.

"I heard what you said to him," Kirk said. There was a warmth in his eyes that almost burned Leo with its intensity. "You said you were staying. With me."

"Didn't you know?" Leo breathed. He knew his face was too open, too expressive. He couldn't hide the desperate hope that he felt.

It was time. It was time to say this, to strip himself bare, even if it meant he would be hurt. Even if the others waiting outside would overhear. *Let them.*

Kirk's hands curved around Leo's shoulders as if they were meant to fit there. He said nothing, but his expression was strained and hopeful, tense to the point of fracture.

"I'm staying," Leo said. "As long as you want me."

His voice shook, and he knew his face was showing everything he felt. There was nowhere to hide.

"Always," Kirk said, gripping his shoulders so hard Leo could feel every imprint of his fingers. "*Always.* Leo, I—please—"

His voice gave out, and he kissed Leo

again, hot and wet and desperate, a wordless promise.

Leo sighed and relaxed into his arms.

The kiss melted all the tension between them, leaving him boneless and happy.

He touched Kirk's stubbled jaw with his fingers, stroking his thumb along the strong line of his jaw.

"I'll be here," Leo said softly. "Here with you. I promise."

***

They roared into Silver Springs with Erick bound hand and foot in the back of Kirk's truck, trussed up like a prize turkey going to a fair. Leo rode in the passenger seat, leaning against Kirk just to feel that solid strength against his shoulder.

They had an escort of three motorcyclists in helmets and dark leathers, and it felt almost like a parade.

"What are the rules?" Leo asked Kirk. "About breaking a truce, I mean. What are they going to do about him?"

Kirk shot him a small, rueful grin. "I have no idea."

Leo snorted. "You don't even care. You just want to hand him over to them and get rid of the problem, admit it." Not that he didn't feel the same.

Kirk didn't deny the truth of this. "Most of all, I want him *gone*," he said. "He's threatened you twice now. If he tries it a third time—" Kirk's expression turned grim, and Leo thumped him in the arm.

"Stop that," Leo said firmly. "That's not going to happen. The last thing I want is to see you end up in jail on a manslaughter charge."

Kirk shook his head, but the grip of his hands on the steering wheel eased a little.

He shot Leo an unreadable look. "You wouldn't come visit me?"

Surprised, Leo laughed. "Oh, I'd come visit you." He lowered his voice, deliberately letting it go husky. "I'd come *visit* you all the time. The guards would strip-search me, and I would walk into your cell naked, smelling of them, with their touch and scent all over me. You wouldn't be able to stop yourself—"

"Jesus," Kirk breathed. He gave the steering wheel a sharp wrench as they rounded a corner. "You're a menace."

"A terrible menace," Leo agreed, grinning. "Maybe I'm the one who needs to be locked up." *My father would probably agree*, Leo thought, and winced. Suddenly it wasn't so funny.

Kirk picked up on it instantly, of course. That was the trouble with werewolves: they picked up on *everything*. "What?"

"I—no, it's nothing."

Kirk gave him a pointedly dubious look, but he didn't force Leo to elaborate.

They drove past the prosperous town and up into the hills again, and Leo tried to distract himself by staring out the window. It was beautiful countryside, the forest blazing with color and the river winding below like a great silver serpent.

"Where are we going?" he asked at last. He couldn't see any houses on either side of the road.

"Werewolf castle," Kirk said.

Leo blinked at him. "Sorry, *what* did you say?"

Kirk's mouth quirked into a half-hidden grin. "Wait until you see it."

***

They walked up the stairs and into the Ridge House hallway, with Kirk carrying Erick over his shoulder. Erick kicked a lot, but Kirk shrugged off the impact of his feet against his back as if they were mosquito bites.

When they entered the huge open living room of the villa, Kirk heard Leo gasp, and he smiled to himself.

"Wow," Leo muttered. He rushed over to the enormous glass wall to look out at the view below. "Oh, that's gorgeous."

Kirk unceremoniously dropped Erick in front of the fireplace. "Stay there," he told him, and Erick glared mutely up at him. One of the werewolves had gagged him with a luggage strap, so that he couldn't even try to use the power of his voice. He was bound hand and foot with rope knots that only tightened the more he struggled. It was a satisfying sight, Kirk had to admit.

He strode over to Leo, who was still mesmerized by the view.

"Can you see the cabin from here?" Leo asked.

Kirk dropped an arm around his shoulder. He couldn't help himself. He had to keep touching Leo, had to keep reminding himself that this was real, that Leo had promised to stay. "Yeah, it's over there." He pointed, far into the distance. "You can just see the chimney."

Leo squinted, sighting along his arm, then shook his head. "I can't see a thing." He turned his head, smiling up at Kirk. "But I thought you probably could."

Warmth filled Kirk's chest to

overflowing. He couldn't resist the impulse to claim a quick kiss from that lovely, smiling mouth.

Leo melted into him, and the kiss deepened until Kirk had to close his eyes. They clung to each other, and Leo made a pleased, happy sound, low in his throat, that Kirk felt all the way down to his bones.

If only they were alone.

But behind them, the room was filling with people, walking with that peculiar soft, loping stride of the werewolf.

Kirk recognized them by their scents. It was the full pack. Some were coming in from Silver Springs, where they'd been working security, and some had been in the house already, probably preparing for night shift.

Kirk turned around, but he didn't let go of Leo. He kept his arms protectively crossed over Leo's chest.

Leo flushed a little, his ears going a delicate shade of pink, but he didn't move away. He let Kirk turn them both around until they faced the crowd.

The werewolves were all dressed in the same security gear Brand wore, in all black, with fitted bulletproof vests. Their faces were serious, intent. They stood around Erick, looking down at him. Some of them looked angry.

With effortless ease, Brand drew all eyes to him as he stepped into the circle of werewolves surrounding Erick. It instantly widened, making room for him.

"We are the pack," he said, his low, rich voice rolling around the room and up into the rafters. "We live by our rules. There is no room for liars or oathbreakers here."

An answering growl ran around the room.

Kirk held back. He kept standing by the window, his arms around Leo, and didn't move to join the circle. He wasn't a full member of the pack. He was an ally, not a subordinate. And if this turned into a full-on brawl, his first responsibility was not to join them, but to get Leo out of here.

"Erick," Brand said. "You broke the truce and entered Kirk's territory. You attempted to steal Kirk's mate. You tried to suborn him with the power of your voice."

Erick shook his head, grunting something beneath the gag.

Brand motioned to Stepan, the tall grizzled man Kirk had seen before. He seemed to be Brand's second in command now.

Stepan stepped forward and knelt to untie Erick's gag. As soon as it was loose, he stepped back again, into the circle.

"Do you have anything to say for yourself?" Brand said. His voice was gentle, but power rolled underneath it like a gathering thunderstorm.

Erick raised his head, blond hair falling over one shoulder. He looked angry and a little disheveled, but his movements were still elegant as he stretched out a long hand, pointing.

"My fellow wolves," Erick said. He sounded calm, reasonable. "Why is there a human here, watching us? What does a human have to do with the councils of the wolf pack?"

Kirk's shoulders tensed, and he felt Leo stiffen in his arms. Some of the younger wolves turned their heads, giving them both hostile looks. Didn't they realize how easily, how expertly they were being manipulated?

"He's using the voice," Leo breathed.

His words were so soft that they were almost inaudible, but not to Kirk. Nor to every other werewolf in the room. He could almost see their ears prick up.

"You're using your gift against us," said Stepan, in a cool voice full of disdain. "You're trying to pull attention away from yourself."

"He's right, though!" said one of the younger wolves, shaking his head as if trying to get rid of some confusion. "We should *not* have a human here. It's an insult."

"You're speaking about my *mate*," Kirk said. He didn't raise his voice. He didn't even step forward. But several of the younger wolves took a step back, including the one who had spoken. "I claimed him in front of all of you," Kirk added, slowly, letting his words sink in. "If you challenge that claim, then let me hear you say it."

There was a dead silence.

The young werewolf turned pale. He

didn't back down completely: his body language was still belligerent, and his hands were knotted into fists. But he bit his lower lip and stayed silent.

Kirk kept staring at him, frowning fiercely. There was no room for half-hearted apologies here. It was all or nothing: fight, or surrender. *Conquer or die*, as his ancestors had once believed.

Slowly, reluctantly, the young werewolf's shoulders relaxed. His hands unknotted. His head dipped back, and he showed Kirk the long pale column of his throat.

Brand nodded at Kirk, and the tension eased just a little. A challenge had been averted.

Now, the wolves turned back to Erick, who sat silently on the floor, smirking a little.

"Do you offer any argument in your own defense?" Brand asked him formally.

In the waiting silence, Erick turned his head, looking directly at Kirk, then at Leo. It was a cold, poisonous look, like the sting of a viper.

"There is nothing I need to defend," Erick

said coolly. "The outsider and his human are no part of us. They do not concern us. They do not fall within the rule of the pack: therefore they are prey."

"You don't decide on pack rule, you arrogant piece of—" one of the older wolves said, and several others chimed in. The mood was turning angry and offended. Erick was losing his audience.

"Enough," Brand said, in that rolling, mellifluous voice.

Instantly, the angry voices stilled. Everyone turned to him, waiting for his verdict.

"You broke the rules, and offer no defense," Brand said slowly. "You create discord within the pack and without. You will be punished."

Now the silence was heavy, expectant.

"Jack, Stepan," Brand said, nodding to them. "Hold him down and strip him."

At this, Erick's head came up. "What are you—" he protested. His arms and legs were still bound, but Jack and Stepan were already untying him. Then they stripped him of his clothes with swift efficiency.

"You lose rank in the pack," Brand told him. "*All* rank. If you want to stay in the pack, you will be lowest of the low. You will submit to anyone and everyone. You will follow every order you are given. You may not speak unless spoken to. You may not eat until all others have eaten their fill. And you will let anyone mount you at their pleasure."

Erick gasped with indignation. "What! You can't—"

"Or you may choose to leave," Brand continued as if he hadn't spoken. "Banishment from the pack and any territory we occupy. Or servitude. Your choice."

For a long moment, Erick visibly hesitated. His pale blue eyes were wide and disbelieving, as if he hadn't thought that this could ever happen to him. As if he didn't think his actions could have consequences.

Kirk watched him, his arms still folded protectively about Leo. He didn't trust Erick, and would prefer him to get himself gone, but he understood Brand's verdict. *Keep your friends close, and your enemies closer.*

He also knew that this wasn't an easy choice. Not for a werewolf.

He'd had a taste of that himself. The sense of belonging that came with being in a pack was incredibly powerful. It felt like coming home.

For Kirk, it was still an uneasy balance. He loved to run with the pack on the days of the full moon, yet he didn't want to be tied to them for the rest of the month. After being a loner for so long, it was too much. Too overwhelming.

He tightened his arms around Leo. *You're the only one I want to be tied to.*

Erick looked up, with a swift hard glance like an arrow. Then that gaze transformed into something softer, meeker. Subservient. "I will stay."

"Good," Brand said, his voice and bearing neutral. Not welcoming, not rejecting.

He doesn't trust him as far as he could throw him, Kirk thought. *Good.* He had a feeling Brand could handle Erick. Especially since Erick's voice didn't seem to work on him.

"Get up," Brand told Erick, who still knelt

in the middle of the circle, naked. "You can start by serving drinks."

Erick opened his mouth as if to protest, and everyone in the circle tensed.

Then Erick's shoulders dropped in defeat, and his mouth snapped shut. He began to stand up, unfolding himself slowly and gracefully. He made no attempt to hide his nudity. Instead, he made a deliberately elegant picture as he slowly walked out of the circle and left the room.

The tension lessened perceptibly as soon as Erick disappeared through the doorway.

In Kirk's arms, Leo twisted, turning around to face Kirk. His face was very grave.

"That's not what I thought would happen," Leo said softly.

"Me either," Kirk had to admit. He'd thought there would be a fight. This seemed very...well, not exactly civilized..but not wolf-like, either. Or maybe it *was*. Maybe this was what happened to a wolf who made a bid for leadership and failed. Maybe a wolf like that was either cast out or reduced to the lowest rank, fighting for bones and scraps of meat. Or scraps of attention, in Erick's case.

"I don't think they're done yet, though," Leo said, looking thoughtful and a little worried.

Kirk lifted his eyebrows. "Done?"

This wouldn't be *done* until Erick somehow found a way to regain his status within the pack. And that could take a very long time.

Before Leo could answer him, Erick came back, carrying a large tray full of glasses and bottles. They didn't clink; he was walking too carefully for that.

Then he knelt, still with that inhuman grace, in front of Brand. He lifted the tray above his head, stretching out his long arms.

Brand nodded. He looked perfectly at ease as he poured himself another drink. As if he was used to having a naked werewolf serve him like this.

Some of the other werewolves laughed, but Brand shot them a look, and they swallowed their laughter. Instead, the group began to talk among themselves, making conversation about their security work. They talked over Erick's head as if he wasn't there, while he knelt to serve every werewolf with his drink of choice.

Some of them touched him. They ran a casual hand through his long blond hair as they poured themselves whiskey, or palmed his shoulder blade, or stroked down the long knobbed ridge of his spine.

"They're testing him," Kirk said to Leo, speaking as softly as he could. He could feel that Leo was tensing up in his arms, wary.

"Why?" Leo said.

"To see if he'll break," Kirk said softly. "Trust is everything here. Nobody trusts him now. He has to keep his word, or be exiled." If Erick couldn't prove that he could take being the lowest in rank, his exit would be swift and sudden.

They both watched as one of the wolves slammed a bottle of vodka down on the tray, hard. The tray wobbled, and Erick had to shift his balance quickly to try and keep the bottles from tipping over. He was on his knees, and it wasn't easy for him to distribute the weight of the tray. One of the glasses toppled, nearly falling off the tray.

In that moment of imbalance, one of the older wolves stepped forward and caught the glass. It was Mike, a curly-haired man with tattoos all over his body. He was one of the three that Brand had trusted to capture Erick, and he was big, muscular, with the look of an ex-marine.

Kirk watched as Mike put the glass back on the tray. Then he laid his massive red-knuckled hand on Erick's shoulder. Mike didn't speak; he merely exchanged a look with Erick.

The tension in the room ratcheted up a notch. All the other werewolves were watching what was happening between Mike and Erick, and the makeshift conversation died down.

Leo twitched in his arms. "Where does it stop?" he asked quietly.

"I don't think it does," Kirk told him.

He watched his fellow werewolves, recognizing the predatory gleam in their eyes.

Some of them had sided with Erick before this. They had something to prove, now. They had to show Brand whose side they were on.

Erick bowed his head in submission and assent. Then he put the tray down onto the carpet and knelt beside it, looking up at Mike through the fall of his long blond hair.

A sharp sound ripped through the waiting, expectant silence.

It was Mike, pulling down the zipper of his jeans.

"*Jesus*," Leo said. His heartbeat was increasing; he was in distress. "Kirk, I—" He shifted in Kirk's arms, looking up at him pleadingly. "I don't want to be here for this," he whispered. "Whatever this is."

Kirk wrapped his arms tightly around Leo, reassuring him. Over Leo's head, he met Brand's eyes.

Words weren't necessary. Brand would have heard everything.

They weren't part of the pack: they could stay and witness this, or they could go. But Kirk would do Brand the courtesy of asking him first. This was his territory, after all.

Kirk signalled with his eyes, looking up and left, toward the place where he wanted to take Leo.

Brand gave him a tiny nod.

They left silently, without looking back. Not even when Erick began to moan.

*****

The stairway to the Ridge House tower creaked under their feet. It seemed older than the rest of the house, and the stairs were massive wooden beams.

As they climbed, Kirk kept his arm tight around Leo's shoulders, protectively, possessively. He couldn't help himself. He wanted Leo by his side forever.

"This is all very gothic," Leo said, his lips curling into an irrepressible grin. "Are you taking me up to a secret chamber with a giant four-poster bed?" His mood had lightened as soon as they left the wolf pack to their own affairs, and Kirk was glad to see it. He didn't want Erick's troubles coming between them.

"Something like that," Kirk said.

Leo made a sound in the back of his throat that sounded like *argh*. "You're not going to tell me, are you."

"Just a few more steps and you'll see for yourself," Kirk promised.

"Fine. But you better be taking me up here to ravish me."

Kirk swallowed, his throat suddenly drawing tight. A bolt of desire shot through him, sudden and vivid and all-consuming. How could Leo do this to him, with nothing but a few words?

Leo looked up at him, smiling. Whatever he saw in Kirk's face seemed to satisfy him. He gave a little sigh. "Ah. Good."

More steps, more creaking, and then they were at the top. In front of them, a heavy oak door loomed.

"*Really* very gothic," Leo commented.

Kirk tried the wrought iron handle. The door swung open easily.

When he stepped into the room, Leo gasped just as he'd done when he first saw the huge wall of glass in the Ridge House living room. "Oh my."

Kirk smiled a little, satisfied with his reaction. The tower was even better than he'd hoped.

All around the room, tall windows reached up to the rafters. It was growing dark outside, but the view was still amazing. The forest stretched to the horizon, interrupted here and there by the silver bends of the river and half-hidden stretches of road. It felt almost like being an eagle, perched high in the mountains to watch the world below.

The floor was dark stone, and most of it was taken up by a sunken bath big enough to fit ten people. There was a slatted wooden cover over it, with rope handles near the edge.

Kirk gripped the handles. The cover could be rolled up like a mat, and he did just that, revealing an expanse of dark, steaming, fragrant water.

"This is unbelievable," Leo said. His eyes were wide, and in the dim golden light from the wall sconces, he looked like a wanton dream, too beautiful to be real.

Kirk swallowed hard, watching him.

"How did you know I was dreaming of a bath when I got home?" Leo said. He ran a hand over the smooth stone edge of the tub. "Wow. It even smells amazing."

Kirk had to agree. The water smelled of minerals, as well as some faint, pleasantly woody scent: sandalwood or maybe cedar. It was mountain water, pure and clear, fresh from some hidden spring.

Suddenly, facing Leo, Kirk felt strangely awkward. Maybe it was because he wanted him so much. It was still hard to believe that Leo was going to stay. *I don't deserve you.*

Even with all his clothes on, he felt more naked than he ever had before.

"Come on," Leo said softly. He was watching Kirk with those wide eyes as though he could see straight through him.

Maybe he could.

With easy, graceful movements, Leo started to undress.

Kirk stared for a long moment, forgetting

everything else. He was mesmerized by Leo's hands, the way they moved, how easily his jeans slipped down his thighs...

"Kirk," Leo said gently. His mouth was still, but his eyes were laughing. "You promised me something."

"Mmm?" Kirk said. He was paying attention to what Leo was saying, really he was. Any minute now, he would start to listen.

Leo kicked his jeans away and began to unbutton his shirt. "Just now. Remember?"

Kirk couldn't remember a thing. He could only watch as Leo's deft fingers bared more of his bare skin. He was hungry, so hungry, for a taste of that skin. He wanted to lick Leo all over.

Finally, Leo dropped his boxers. Fully nude, he slid into Kirk's arms.

Tugging at his hair to bring down Kirk's head, Leo whispered into Kirk's ear, "You promised you'd ravish me."

Kirk's heart skipped a beat, and he had to close his eyes and just *feel* Leo's warmth against his.

Don't let this moment end.

He slipped his arms around Leo, holding him close.

"I never promised that," Kirk said, trying to disguise the rush of affection and need in his voice. Trying for casual. He didn't even know who he was trying to fool, Leo or himself.

Leo stepped back and shook his head as if disappointed. "Oh?" he said archly. "Must have been some other werewolf."

Kirk didn't have a comeback for that. In fact, he had to bite back a stab of jealousy. *What other werewolf? Who dares—*

Leo smirked, satisfied at his reaction. "If you want me," Leo said in a soft, sensual, infinitely seductive voice, "you'd better get into the water."

With that last word, he slipped into the bath, so smoothly that the water barely rippled around him. "Oh *god*, that's good," Leo said huskily. He spread his arms, floating. The water lapped at his shoulders. "I needed this so *much*..." He groaned with pleasure.

Kirk couldn't take another second of this.

Here he was, standing at the edge of the bath still fully dressed, like an idiot, while Leo was lying back in the water like an offering, tipping his head back to shamelessly expose the delicious line of his throat, and making *sex noises*.

He ripped off his clothes, with more violent hurry than grace.

A button pinged into a corner.

Kirk didn't care.

All he cared about was Leo, lying there in the dark water, his body shimmering in the golden light.

Waiting for him.

***

Leo exhaled, slowly and luxuriously. His very bones were melting, dissolving in the hot water. Steam was rising from his wet skin, and he could feel the flush of heat all the way up to his ears.

And Kirk was watching him. Kirk was almost bare, except for one sock and an undershirt, and he seemed to be having some trouble getting rid of those last two obstacles.

Kirk's hands were shaking, and he was watching Leo.

Leo leaned back in the water and watched him in return. It was a rush, there was no denying that. He had *power* over Kirk, over this immensely strong, powerful, obstinate, wonderful man. He could bring him to his knees, if he chose.

He winced. A sudden image of Erick being forced to his knees stabbed at his memory.

Don't think about that.

Leo didn't even like Erick, and he hated the way Erick had treated him. Like prey, like some kind of trinket Erick wanted to possess and then discard. But he didn't like the way the wolf pack were treating Erick, either.

He deserves to be punished, Leo told himself. *The pack has rules, and he needs to keep them. That's the way it should be.* But to a mere human like Leo, the pack rules could easily seem cruel.

Kirk had sensed his distraction. He had slid into the water without Leo even noticing, and now he was moving in, his eyes dark and intent, his arms reaching out for Leo.

Leo slid into his arms, needing that comfort more than sex, just for a moment. Needing *him*.

"Don't worry so much," Kirk said, that deep voice rumbling into his ear. "It's like you, to care even for your enemies. But there's no need."

Leo sighed. He couldn't deny that he was distracted, no more than he could stop breathing.

Kirk stroked his hair with one wet palm, smoothing it back. It felt good. Calming.

"I can hear them, if I focus," Kirk told him. "Trust me. Don't worry."

Leo nodded reluctantly. He had to believe that. And he did trust Kirk, always.

Kirk's big hand moved down his scalp, a firm touch that made Leo want to purr and push into it like a cat.

With another sigh, Leo surrendered himself into Kirk's hands. It was time to stop thinking. It was time to be here, to be with Kirk, and let himself *feel*.

***

Leo lay back in the steaming water again, feeling it lap about his shoulders.

He was floating. The bath was so big that he could lie here feeling weightless, not even his feet touching the bottom.

But Kirk's hands were on his hips, steadying him.

Stroking him. Big, warm hands, gliding over his skin.

At first it felt soothing, and then Leo's skin started to tingle, little electric thrills that went straight to his cock. "Mmm. Oh, that feels good."

"Oh yeah?" Kirk said, and his voice was

low, dark. Promising.

Leo shivered a little, deliciously. He let his legs fall open on either side of Kirk. He was so hard already, and he wanted Kirk to see it.

Kirk growled low in his throat. By now Leo was so attuned to him that he could tell the difference between those growls. This wasn't threat or anger or warning; this was a sound of pure arousal, a sound that Kirk couldn't help making.

That sound made heat and desire bloom in Leo, like a rose in sunlight. He thrust up into the air, making the water ripple and splash over the sides.

Then he met Kirk's eyes, and the heat he saw there almost burned him.

Kirk's hand gripped his hips, tugging him closer, and he floated over to Kirk like a leaf on a stream.

Leo legs closed around Kirk's broad, strong back, and he sighed and let his head tip deeper into the water.

Kirk bent forward and licked him, a warm wet stripe all the way up to the tip of his cock.

Leo moaned, loudly. He just hoped the werewolves on the floor below weren't listening, because he couldn't help himself.

"You—always want to lick me," he said, trying to make it sound like a complaint. It really wasn't.

Almost hidden by the heavy stubble, Kirk's mouth twitched in a small grin.

"You're right," he said. "I do."

And he proved it with another long lick up Leo's cock. Slower this time, hotter. Tasting Leo as if he was a delicious dessert.

Leo moaned again, and then he lifted his arms above his head to grip the edge of the huge bath. He needed the support.

Kirk's big hands stroked his chest, making a little detour to circle his nipples. He knew how sensitive Leo was there, and he made full use of that knowledge, teasing and tormenting until his nipples stood up stiffly, aching to be touched again.

That's the trouble with werewolves, Leo

thought. *You can't hide a thing from them.*

He shoved himself back into Kirk, demanding more. Demanding attention for the very visible evidence of his arousal.

Slowly, teasingly, Kirk switched his grip, moving his hands around and below until he gripped Leo's ass.

"Oh," Leo moaned, pressing back into those strong hands. "Oh, please—" He was throbbing, eager to be touched, but he didn't want his own hands on himself.

Kirk's dark eyebrows lifted. "Please what?"

Leo bit back a curse. If Kirk wanted to tease, if Kirk wanted him to beg, then he was going to get his wish.

"Please touch me," Leo said, letting his voice go husky and soft.

He knew he was blushing, all the way up to the tips of his ears, but he also knew how much Kirk loved it when he talked like this.

"Please," Leo repeated, looking up at Kirk from under his eyelashes. "Take me into your mouth. Suck me until I come, make me spill inside you, please—"

Kirk's hands closed tighter on his ass, kneading him. He looked wild, with his long dark hair unbound and spilling over his shoulders, and his eyes dark with hunger.

For a moment, their eyes met, a breathless stare meeting untamed arousal.

Then Kirk bent forward again, and this time he sucked Leo right into his mouth.

Leo gasped, and his hands clenched around the stone edge of the bath.

God, this felt so good. Kirk's mouth was hot and strong and wet, sucking him in so hard that Leo could almost feel himself lifting out of the water.

"Yes, do it," he urged Kirk on breathlessly, writhing in his hands, shamelessly pushing himself closer, deeper. "Do it, suck me —"

Kirk hummed under his breath, creating distracting and delicious vibrations that traveled all the way up Leo's spine. And he obeyed.

"Oh," Leo moaned, helpless and so turned on he could barely breathe. It was like having a tiger on a leash, to have Kirk obeying him like this, his head bent to Leo's service.

Kirk sucked Leo down with such eager skill, his tongue curling wetly around the head, swallowing around him as if he was trying to devour Leo whole.

"I can't—oh god, I can't last—" Leo tried to say, but now words were deserting him too. His breath was stuttering, and his whole body was caught up in the fast rhythm Kirk set for him.

Thrills of pleasure shook him, and he grabbed the edge of the bath so hard that his fingers turned white. "I—I'm going to—"

His hips thrust up, stuttering once, twice, three times—and then he was coming so hard that he nearly blacked out. Kirk swallowed around him as he came, pulling his pleasure from him, *demanding* it.

All Leo could do was give in to that demand.

The pinnacle of pleasure lasted for a long while, and it left him feeling blissed out and incredibly light, as light as a feather floating on air.

Leo lay back in the steaming water with a sigh.

Then Kirk lifted his head and licked his lips, giving him a look that was so smug and satisfied that Leo had to laugh.

"You look very proud of yourself," Leo said fondly. *Like the cat that got the cream.*

Kirk's eyes crinkled at the corners, a hidden smile. "I like seeing you come apart like that."

Now Leo's blush was turning fiery indeed, like an old iron stove heating to cherry-red. "You do that to me," he whispered.

Kirk ducked his head, his long hair hiding his expression for a moment. He pulled Leo closer, his arms locking around Leo's back. Then they were pressed together in a tight embrace.

Leo sighed with pleasure, feeling Kirk's strength all around him, holding him so warm and safe. "I love you so much," he whispered.

Then he sucked in a breath, shocked. He hadn't meant to just...let it slip out like that. The words felt like stones, dropping into the water with heavy thunks.

Worried, Leo glanced up at Kirk, trying to gauge his reaction.

What he saw took his breath away.

Kirk's eyes were wide and very dark, and his mouth was slightly open. He looked more vulnerable than Leo had ever seen him. He looked as if someone had given him a present so enormous that he didn't even know what to do with it.

"Kirk?" Leo breathed, and he laid a hand along the rough stubble of his jaw.

Kirk looked down at him, and he gave a great sigh.

His arms wrapped around Leo's shoulders, solid and warm and real. Then Kirk bent closer, his stubble scraping Leo's cheek, and he said in Leo's ear, "Stay with me?"

His voice was in its lowest register, gravelly and rough, but to Leo it sounded like music.

"I will," Leo said, and he turned his head to kiss Kirk's cheek. "I will. As long as you want me."

He'd said this once already, he knew, but he needed to say it again. He needed to hear Kirk reply, he needed that affirmation. And Kirk seemed to need it just as much.

Kirk nuzzled Leo's cheek, then his neck. "Always," he breathed. "Oh, sweetheart—"

Hearing that word on Kirk's lips gave Leo such a warm fuzzy feeling, he almost felt embarrassed for himself. Almost, but not quite.

"I'm your mate," Leo whispered reassuringly, stroking Kirk's cheek again. "You said so yourself."

Kirk sighed and relaxed, as if a great weight had lifted off his shoulders. "And I'm yours," he said roughly, his eyes half-shut as if he thought the words would come easier that way. "I'm yours."

Then he buried his hands in Leo's hair and kissed him.

Leo melted into the kiss, wrapping himself around Kirk. The water lapped around the both of them, warm and close, and it felt as though they were alone together in some tropical ocean. Nothing else existed but the two of them.

Kirk moaned, low in his throat, and the kiss deepened. His tongue was slick and thrust deep into Leo, rough and passionate and urgent.

Leo shuddered. *Yes. Do it. Whatever you want. Don't hold back.* He tried to communicate without words, with only the softness of his mouth and the eager tip of his tongue.

Then he remembered the one sure way to show Kirk how he felt, with no chance of misunderstandings.

And if it happened to drive Kirk wild at the same time...well. He wasn't going to object to that.

He tipped his head back, slowly and deliberately exposing his throat.

***

Kirk heard himself growl, and he knew all the restraints had just come off.

With Leo's deliberate submission, his deliberate provocation, the mood had changed in an instant. From warm tender feeling to shocking, brutal *need.*

Kirk felt fire licking at his bones. He needed to have Leo, he needed to be inside him right *now.*

His heart twisted inside him, warning him that this was *Leo,* this was his love, he should go slow, be careful, gentle—he couldn't—

But the wolf wasn't listening.

The wolf knew what he wanted, better than he did.

And so, it appeared, did Leo.

Even as Kirk wrestled with himself, Leo was looking at him from beneath his eyelashes. A sultry look, full of waiting hunger.

"Erick said that you like to have an audience," Leo said softly. "He was trying to hurt me, of course. But maybe he was right. Maybe we should go below, invite the other wolves to come and watch. Would you like that?"

Kirk ground his teeth, repressing the outraged voice inside his head that shouted *No* and *You're mine*.

He was *not* going to give in to Leo that easily. He wasn't going to rise to the bait.

Even if a part of him *was* rising. A very visible part, that throbbed in rhythm with his heartbeat.

Leo stroked his own chest, rubbing at his wet skin, his pink little nipples. "It's not like they haven't watched us before," he said softly. "When you claimed me."

He was doing this deliberately, stirring up those memories Kirk tried to keep buried. He wasn't proud of them. He didn't want to be like that—nothing but fire and need and driving, desperate instinct.

But apparently, Leo wanted him like this.

Leo wanted *all* of him.

Kirk could see the truth of that in Leo's expression, so open, so ready for him and unafraid. And he could smell the truth of it in Leo's luscious scent, rising over the scented water and into his nostrils like a breath of pure lust.

He waded forward, deeper into the hot water, carrying them both.

Leo's eyes widened when Kirk's hands clamped down on Leo's wet thighs. He pushed Leo up against the rounded edge of the bath.

"So you want all of them to watch, do you?" Kirk said, his voice a low growl that twisted the words, making them sound darker. "You want them all to fuck you, too? Would you roll over and let them have you?"

He could see it, the spark in Leo's eyes that caught fire as he watched Kirk loom over him. It was hot, urgent, demanding.

If Leo wanted him like this, then Leo would get his wish.

"I would," Leo claimed brazenly, licking his bottom lip with the tip of his pink wet tongue. "I'd spread my legs for them and bend over—make them see me, make them touch me —and then I'd make you watch—"

That image was enough to fan the flames higher. They burned up into Kirk's throat, taking his voice away from him until he could only groan with need. He was harder than steel.

Roughly, Kirk slipped a finger into Leo, testing him. He wasn't gentle now; he wasn't kind. If Leo wanted kindness from him, he wouldn't have started this.

Leo was tight, so damn tight, clinging to him.

"You're not even ready," Kirk accused him. He added another finger, watching Leo bite back a moan, watching the flush spread all the way down to his chest. "You couldn't take it, not without me to—open you—"

He had to stop talking then, had to concentrate on what he was doing.

Three fingers.

Too fast, too soon. He knew Leo was feeling the burn of it.

But Leo was urging him on with breathless cries, little gasping moans that seemed to be driven out of him with every thrust of Kirk's thick fingers.

"Spread your legs," Kirk told him, harsh. "Open wide for me."

Leo moaned harder, but he did as he was told. He spread his legs, clutching his knees to make himself open up wider. He was half leaning against the stone lip of the bath, half floating in the water, with only Kirk's hands to hold him up from drowning.

He felt the tight muscle clamp down on his fingers, watched Leo bite his bottom lip and swear voicelessly.

It felt good. Every tiny thrust of his fingers made Leo moan and shiver and swear. And he was hot inside, so hot and velvety—he knew how good it would feel on his cock—

With another bitten-off curse, Leo flung an arm over the edge of the bath and scrabbled around, hunting for something. Kirk couldn't tear his eyes away to look.

But then Leo's hand returned in his field of view, waving something. A bottle of bath oil.

Kirk met Leo's eyes. "You want me to slick you up? You think you're ready to take my cock?"

Leo's eyes were wide, and the pupils were huge, almost eclipsing the black. His scent rose off him in waves, intense enough to lure werewolves for miles around. But Kirk was the only one who would catch him. The only one who would have him.

"Yes," Leo whispered.

Kirk teased the swollen rim of his opening with his thumb, making Leo moan again. "Say it, then."

"Please," Leo moaned.

For once the roles were reversed, Kirk thought. Leo was usually the talkative one, the vocal one. But right now he didn't seem capable of using words of more than one syllable, and Kirk...Kirk was enjoying the hell out of seeing him like this.

"Please what?" he asked, letting his thumb slide over Leo's half-hard cock while his fingers worked deeper inside. He was still so tight—it would be a struggle. But Leo seemed to want it more than anything.

"Please—" Leo rolled his head against the stone, his long eyelashes fluttering. "Oil me, so you can—oh, god, do that again—so you can take me. Put your—oh—your cock in me—"

His voice was breathless, his cheeks were flushed, and his scent rose in heated clouds. Everything he did spoke of longing and urgency.

So Kirk did as he was asked, tipping the bottle into his hand and letting the scented oil coat his fingers.

But he did it very, very slowly.

Leo fought him all the way, rolling his hips, swearing at him and trying to make him go faster.

Kirk mouthed kisses into his neck, tasting the sweetness of his skin. Oil dripped from his fingers and into the water, adding to the orgy of scent: spruce, a little musk, sandalwood.

Oh, but Leo was lovely, to all his senses. The arch of his back, the warm salt of his sweat, the muttered curses and moans that dripped from his lips, and the fierce tight clench of his body on Kirk's fingers...he would never get enough of this. Never.

He looked down to see his fingers disappear into Leo, oil spreading from his touch in gleaming concentric circles, and then he slipped them out. Slowly, enjoying the feeling of it, watching Leo's reaction.

"Please," Leo begged, moaning when he felt Kirk's fingers leave him. "Don't stop now—"

Kirk ran his fingers down the smooth, bare skin of his chest, leaving a gleaming trail behind.

"Are you mine?" he asked, low and rough.

"Yes," Leo said instantly, his words almost falling over themselves. "Yes, god yes, I'm yours—do it—"

That was enough. Kirk lined up his hard length and began to press inside him, feeling the strain of it, the incredible tightness that gripped his cock.

Leo's head tipped back and he moaned again, soft and urgent. His hands gripped Kirk's shoulders, holding onto him for dear life.

The oil made Kirk's hands very slick, and it was hard to keep a grip on himself. And Leo was clenching around him like a velvet fist, almost pushing him out, so that he had to use greater force.

He closed his eyes for a moment, concentrating on pressing inside, feeling the swollen rim stretch and resist in pulses. One of Leo's hands strayed into his hair, pulling, and the sting of pain only added to Kirk's hard-won pleasure.

It was tight, tight to the point of pain— Leo's body seemed intent on fighting him, despite the work of his fingers. But Kirk was unstoppable now. He could go slow, using all the discipline he had left, but he could not stop, not now. He pressed on, shoving into Leo with relentless strength, holding him down by the hips and pressing him up against the stone lip of the bath until he folded open like a flower.

"Take it," Kirk grunted, feeling the vicious clench ease just a little. He ground into Leo, pushing deeper.

Leo's thighs twitched and trembled, and his mouth was lush and swollen. Kirk bent and kissed him again, licking at his lips, then biting him. He wanted everything. He wanted to *bite* and *own* and *mark* and *claim*.

Leo was his, to do with as he pleased.

Leo was *his*.

And he was Leo's.

Oh, it went both ways. It was surrender as much as it was battle, this need to drive himself deeper, to own Leo for the space of a breath, to connect them as closely as he could. He wanted to be inside—so deep inside.

Leo groaned, his fingertips grazing Kirk's shoulder, then pushing into his hair again. He seemed to have a fascination for Kirk's hair.

Kirk drove into him, urging his reluctant, struggling body to give in, to give up, to submit to him.

Let me in.

Let me have you.

Leo's thighs were pressed back almost against his chest, and he was holding himself open for Kirk's pleasure. Water splashed around them as Kirk moved, lifting Leo's hips, pulling him closer so his cock could plunge deeper. Still his body resisted, and Kirk was only halfway inside him.

"Breathe," Kirk muttered, seeing Leo's face turn rosy with effort. "Breathe, push back-"

"Shut up," Leo said.

Kirk sucked in a breath, almost shocked, and stopped moving.

Leo smiled up into Kirk's eyes. It wasn't a sweet smile, oh no; it was sharp, a biting smile, almost vicious. The kind of smile a fox would wear, upon seeing its prey come near.

"Stop coddling me," Leo ordered him, "and fuck me."

Kirk breathed hard. He felt Leo deliberately clench down on him: once, twice, a firm vicious grip that made him see stars.

Then Kirk began to move.

Leo wailed, a thin sound that spiraled higher when Kirk drove him hard into the stone lip of the bath, almost bending him double with the force of his thrust.

He was force, he was power, he was a hammer on the anvil, and he drove himself all the way inside while Leo yelled and moaned and hit him on the shoulders with his fists. That was a signal Kirk knew well by now, and he knew it didn't mean *stop.*

The wolf howled inside his mind, urging him on. *Your mate is wayward. You need to claim him again and again. Show him who owns him.*

Now he was deep inside Leo, his hips flush against Leo's warm thighs. For a moment he stayed there, enjoying the tight clench of him, and the way Leo shuddered on his cock. He was buried in Leo to the hilt, and the burn of his withdrawal made Leo gasp.

Kirk set a rhythm, sliding out then slamming back in, fast and hard and brutal.

His hips struck Leo's body with every hard thrust, and Leo grunted with the impact, but at the same time he was saying "Yes—do it— oh—" and lifting himself higher, tilting his hips toward Kirk in a plea for more. He was so eager, so desperate to be used.

"Leo," Kirk groaned when he drove forward again, so deep. There were no other words left in him but his mate's name.

Nothing existed but this, the primal rhythm, the scent of musk and heated flesh, and the slick sounds of their bodies slamming together.

Kirk shook his sweat-damp hair back and pulled Leo tight against him, feeling Leo's fingernails dig into his back.

They were so close.

Leo was hard and straining against him, his cock leaving wet trails on Kirk's stomach, and Kirk was snapping his hips now, increasing his speed. The tiny little noises that came from Leo's mouth drove him crazy.

Pleasure built between them, heat and pressure rising.

Leo tipped his head back, gasping for air, and rolled his hips.

Kirk growled, all his muscles tightening for one—last—push—

Leo clutched at his back, gasping for air, and wetness shot up against Kirk's stomach.

Kirk groaned. Heat pooled in his stomach, in his balls, and then surged up and out of him. He held on, shuddering, his hands tight enough on Leo's hips to leave bruises, and came and came and came.

Leo was talking to him in small broken words, mere whispers of sound, telling him how good this was, how amazingly good, how hard and hot Kirk felt inside him, even now.

Kirk shuddered again and again, aftershocks tearing through him like lightning. He held on to Leo for dear life, and felt Leo's hands clench in his hair again.

Every time he thought he was done, another aftershock rocked through them both. They stayed like that for a long while, locked together, until finally the shudders eased and Kirk felt himself relax.

Leo smiled up at him shakily, looking utterly exhausted, but blissful.

Kirk bent his head to kiss him, and Leo responded instantly, melting into him. They breathed in sync, exploring each other's mouths with slow, leisurely touches.

Finally Kirk pulled away, slowly, and Leo unfolded his doubled-up body with a groan.

"I feel wrecked," Leo complained, stretching slowly and letting the water wash over him.

Kirk nodded. "You look like it, too."

Leo shot him a filthy look, and Kirk grinned. He probably looked as wrecked as Leo did. He felt utterly satisfied, warm and glowing.

There was only one more thing he wanted to do.

"Come on," he told Leo softly, and now the tenderness he felt was coming out in his voice, too, unrestrained. "Let's go back to the cabin."

***

A sliver of moon was rising over the forest, and Kirk watched it as he drove. It called to him—it would always call to him—but he ignored that call, focusing instead on the beauty of the soft, silvery light playing over the treetops.

His mind was barely on the road, but he knew the area well enough to drive through it with his eyes closed, and his hands were relaxed and steady on the steering wheel.

Leo was a warm weight against his shoulder. He was fast asleep, though every now and then he murmured something that Kirk couldn't make out, talking in his sleep. Kirk hoped he was dreaming of something good.

Leo's scent was warm, relaxed and peaceful. It drifted into Kirk's nostrils with every breath he took, and he smiled to himself.

He had something in mind, something he wanted to do when they arrived at the cabin.

He wanted to carry Leo inside. For once, Kirk wanted to give way to a romantic impulse.

The first time he'd met Leo, he'd carried him into the cabin, too. But that time Leo had been wounded, and it wasn't exactly a romantic occasion. It was a moment full of pain and fear, and Leo didn't even know who he was.

This time, it would be different.

He could see it in his mind's eye.

He would scoop up Leo's warm, willing weight, and Leo's arms would lock around his neck, his eyes full of trust and love. He'd carry

Leo into his home, and they would start their new life together.

Leo shifted against him, muttering something under his breath.

Kirk dropped a kiss on his golden hair.

"Shhh, sweetheart," he said softly. "We're going home."

Thank you for reading! I'm currently working on a new book in the Mountain Wolves series, **_Wolf Moon_**.

If you'd like to know when it's available, please sign up for my new release e-mail list at eepurl.com/xNp1X

If you enjoyed this story, check out Isabel Dare's other stories on Amazon.com:

Taken by the Minotaur Trilogy
When young prince Theseus enters the Labyrinth, he expects to fight a deadly man-beast monster: half man, half bull. But he does not expect to find the Minotaur aroused and ready for him. And he would never have imagined that the Minotaur would become his mate...

Taken by the Centaurs

Young Orpheus finds himself singing to a herd of eager male Centaurs. He's enjoying his new audience, but when he accidentally gives them wine, he finds out just how dangerous and depraved Centaurs really are.

Used by the Vikings

When Edric dares to refuse the advances of sly Viking troublemaker Leif, he must be punished. He is bound naked to the Great Oak, and from sunrise til sunset, anyone may make public use of him...

Stealing Ganymede

When Zeus assumes the shape of a giant eagle and carries beautiful young Ganymede off to the top of Mount Olympus to seduce him, Ganymede is outraged. What will it take for Zeus to claim him for his own?

Party Favor

On the night of his 21st birthday, Alex gets a code word that allows his boyfriend Jeremy to use him in any way he wants. What Alex doesn't know is that Jeremy is taking him to a night club for his birthday party, and all the guests know the code word, too...

Caught by Scylla

A beautiful but arrogant prince sails too close to the lair of the legendary Scylla. The monstrous being's slick tentacles caress the humiliated prince everywhere, while an entire ship full of sailors watches!

Join Isabel Dare's mailing list at eepurl.com/xNp1X to get updates about new books!

Legal Notice

Printed in Great Britain
by Amazon